JUST PERFECT

Hanne Arts

DEDICATION

This novel is dedicated to my father, who always stands by me during the difficult times and who has fueled my love for reading and writing.

ACKNOWLEDGEMENTS

I would like to express the most profound gratitude to everyone who has helped me produce this novel. I'd especially like to thank all my writing friends, who were incessantly there when I needed them to help search for the perfect word or phrase. Without their guidance my book would not have looked the way it does today.

I would also like to thank my family for always being there for me, supporting me both during the book-writing process as well as during the difficult events and experiences leading up to it.

My gratitude goes out to the people who inspired me to write originally – yes, I'm sure you know who you are – and, had I not been taught and pushed to my potential by you, I might not have found the courage to pursue my bold writing dreams in the way I do today.

Furthermore, a big fat thanks to all the dense, egocentric bastards who thought it fun to beat up and traumatize the little girl I once was. It has made me stronger, so thank you.

An even bigger thanks to all of those who consequently helped me out of the pit I had fallen into.

Thank you to all my readers without whom these words would be meaningless. Though I may pen down the words and scenes, you are the true angels through which the text is infused with meaning.

And lastly, to everyone who has, at one point or another, felt like they didn't belong, yet fought through, or are still fighting, to grace the world with their presence today.

PART ONE

Every thought is a battle,
Every breath is a war,
And I don't think I'm winning anymore
- Unknown

PREFACE

Beep! Beep! Beep! Beep!

I felt myself sinking away, yet I was vaguely aware of people rushing into the room, the scraping sound of machinery being moved, and the rustling of papers being searched. My brain registered shapes shifting in front of my blurred vision, voices mumbling hushed messages.

Beep! Beep! Beep! Beep!

I tried to breathe steadily, but the turmoil in my head wouldn't cooperate with my need for oxygen. My attempts to gulp in air were in vain and a hoarse murmur exited through my opened mouth.

If I must die now, so be it.

It felt like I was drowning. One last time I strove to get my head above water, to scream for help, but the current was too strong. I felt myself being pulled away, slowly being dragged down. My efforts grew weaker as the strength drained out of me, and my fatigued body screamed for me to stop fighting. I let myself be carried off as the waves dragged me under.

CHAPTER ONE

"Hey, Christina!" shouted Cathy, picking up her pace. "Wait for me! Don't walk so fast!"

I turned around and saw my friend rushing toward me, her heels ticking on the tiled marble floor as she clumsily advanced. Her long golden-blonde curls waved behind her like an angel's halo; her big blue eyes stared into the depths of my own like a serpent's stare. She replaced a strand of hair that had escaped from the rest, her long fingernails brushing her pale and smooth skin. I often marveled at her perfection, admired her for it, yet Cathy took it all for granted. I guess she was just lucky. Just perfect.

She steadily narrowed the space between us, shaking her prominent hips gracefully as I allowed her to catch up. She wore a white, low-cut top that barely covered her large breasts, which were enhanced by a blue push-up bra that was visible through the thin fabric. The cool temperature outside didn't seem to bother her, and her mini-skirt floated around her slender legs as she covered the length of the hallway. Not that I was jealous of her or anything, but sometimes I simply longed to be more like her. Stronger. Prettier.

Cathy caught up with me, breathing slightly heavier from the effort. It did not sound laborious or unattractive, however, as it had something sensual, some silky undertone that I could not define. Though I granted her all the fortune in the world, her perfect look often made me uncomfortable about my own clumsy and flat-chested body. The only curve on me was my belly.

As if to rub it in my face further, Cathy threw me one of her dazzling smiles and flipped her hair back nonchalantly. I was certain that all the guys in the hallway had their eyes fixed upon her.

"So, did you do the math homework?" The first thing she said to me. No "hi" or "how are you?" Just whether I did the homework or not. Just like that. Her words mirrored her look completely – dashing, delicate, and straight to the point.

Well, that was just Cathy's way of doing things, and I knew her for long enough to understand this. She most likely already knew the answer forming on my lips that very instant.

"Of course I did the homework," I replied matter-of-factly, but I had gathered that this had not exactly been the question. There had been an underlying statement, and, looking at Cathy, I immediately understood the message hidden in those hard yet pleading eyes; they inevitably displayed what she had originally queried for. Obediently, I opened my schoolbag, took out the math sheet, and handed it to her. Before allowing me a chance to say anything else, she had disappeared to copy it.

I guess that's just the upside of befriending a dweeb, but I didn't mind. After all, I had the right to be in her presence, to chat with her and leave school with her. This was simply the other side of the bargain.

Since she had become popular at the end of middle school it felt like an honor to even have anything to do with her. If in return she asked for my help, I was more than willing to live up to my part of the unspoken pact.

I entered the mathematics classroom and waved briskly at Marc on my way in, a blush spreading over my cheeks. With a wide grin plastered onto his face, he waved back at me while I sat down in my usual seat three rows in front of him, an arrangement we followed in numerous of our other classes as well.

I took out my supplies, placed them neatly on the wooden desk in front of me, and scribbled several figures into my notebook, impatiently waiting for Cathy to return with my handout.

Just as the class was about to commence and the clock's hands neared the two p.m. mark that was to end our lunch hour, she finally rushed in to take her place beside me. My eyes found hers immediately.

"Ohmygod Christina," she whispered under her breath. "Couldn't you have made your math neater? Your handwriting sucks." She pushed the sheet over the smooth surface of the wooden table, giving me a displeased glare.

I held the now-wrinkled paper in my left hand, smoothing out the creases with the palm of my right. Lowering my head slightly, I could smell Cathy's Chanel perfume blushing its edges.

As the bell resounded through the halls, Mr. Wilson took attendance, and I followed his gaze as he scanned the room over the rim of his reading glasses. To calm down the noise of chatter and disorder that had not yet ceased, he stood up from his beige office chair and slammed a heavy calculus textbook on the empty desk at the front of the class. The noise died down at a stroke.

"Today we will cover geometry. The vertices of triangles, to be more precise." He paced back and forth in front of the whiteboard, his hands intertwined behind his back. "Before we begin, however, could everyone please turn in yesterday's homework assignment?"

He covered the area of the room in several brisk steps as the students shuffled through papers to take out the worksheet. There were several excuses of why the item was not present in class, but Mr. Wilson saw through these explanations, no matter how valid, and declared a ten percent deduction for each day it was late. Some of the students groaned.

Cathy did not even grant me as much as a glance as she handed him her sheet. I, too, turned it in, and Mr. Wilson gave it a cursory look.

"Pay more attention to your penmanship in the future," he complained. "It is evident that you did not spend much time on the assignment."

He then moved his attention to Cathy's work, and with a mere nod he marched on toward the front of the class.

"Now, onto triangles," he announced as notebooks were flipped open and pens taken out of their cases.

An hour of concentrated angle calculations later, Cathy and I found ourselves in yet another of our joint classes. Chemistry with Mr. Roberts. Cathy was studiously penning down notes – or maybe it was the last of yesterday's enthalpy calculations – while I took out my papers from my binder and turned around in my chair as if pulled in that direction by a magnetic attraction. My body went weak and time stood still.

"Christina?" Mr. Roberts' voice sliced through the thin air of the room. "Christina, what answer did you get on question two of last night's homework assignment?"

My gaze was cut away from Marc who, seated behind me, could not help but grin as my eyes repeatedly wandered back to him. I looked up abruptly and then reverted my gaze back down to the handout in front of me.

"Number two, you said?" My eyes flew rapidly over the paper. Feeling the other students' heavy glares falling onto my shoulders and sides, I responded within that same breath: "Forty-nine kilojoules, sir."

Mr. Roberts looked down at his sheet and approved with a nod. "Very well." He made his way to the other side of the class and then turned around again. "Very well." His eyes scanned the room for his next victim, singling out Maria.

"Maria. Question three."

Maria's cheeks turned tomato-red as she looked around herself. It had unmistakably been her he had called upon. With shaking hands she thus lifted up her assignment, the paper rustling between her fingers like autumn leaves encountering a strong wind.

"Hu-hund-hundred t-ten." She stuttered as a communal chuckle rose up in the room.

"Hu-hundred ten what?" Mr. Roberts retorted, his arms crossed over his chest as he stood before her.

"Hu-hundred ten kilojoules," Maria stammered in response. The giggles grew thicker. Her speech problem had been a source of mirth for as long as I could remember, and the day she came into school ten minutes late was still pressed into my memory as if tattooed there in dark black ink. As I said, my class was not quite so accepting of her, and the day she was late to school and stuttered her excuse sent a wave of jokes and giggles through the room. She had sat down, her head cowered between hunched shoulders and her eyes twitching while she winced as though in pain. It was confusing to look at, but it all became frighteningly clear when Bob and Andrew strolled into the classroom only moments later. I still don't know what happened, but it sends chills down my spine to even try to visualize what took place at all. Andrew had winked at Arthur, who then held up his thumbs in return.

I have to admit I did feel somewhat sorry for Maria, but I also need to add that I never laughed along. I swear. Furthermore, I never even spoke to her or anything, as she was not only as nimble as a mouse, but she also faded into the background as much as she scurried to leave at the first sound of the bell. I was never able to catch up with her – I never really put in too much effort either – but Bob and Andrew often did. They'd bring their gang – usually made up of themselves, Arthur, and Peter – and Maria would undergo a beating, suffering blows like heavy gusts of wind pounding into her crumpled frame. Today would be no different, and I could feel the leaden air press me down forcefully on my hard plastic seat.

Beside me, Cathy gave me a soft nudge with her elbow, bringing me back to the room. She passed me a piece of paper no bigger than the size of my palm.

Wanna meet up after school? We could see some shops and then go to that club again.

The darkness in my head changed to light and then returned to dark again. I considered her proposal, more than willing to come along even if I disliked the place, but at the same time I realized it was impossible. I had other commitments.

I crumpled up the piece of paper and whispered: "I promised my dad I'd prepare dinner tonight. Sorry."

Her face was a mixture of disappointment and irritation, her sky-blue eyes squinting to thin lines of mascara caterpillars. She placed her hand onto my shoulder, or rather clamped her hand over my shoulder, responding, slightly too loud: "I understand. The situation, I mean. If you change your mind or want to come over later, certainly don't hesitate."

She just about opened her mouth again when Mr. Roberts' ruler fell down hard on our desk, the sound thundering through the room.

"I tolerate no talking during my class," he roared as he placed himself directly in front of us. His legs were spread out wide and his hands were planted on his hips. "Leave that until the end of school."

As if mocking him, just at that moment the bell rang and Cathy flew out of her seat. *Come on*, she mouthed as she pulled me by the hand. In one swift motion I swept up my supplies and, with an apologetic nod in my professor's direction, followed her out the room and to my locker. She gave me air kisses on both cheeks and left to get her own belongings.

I unlocked my locker, pushed several books into my bag, and made my way to the swinging doors, passing Maria on my way. In the corner of my eye I could see her, surrounded by dark shadows of predators, and I could just hear Bob spit several words at her before the others appeared. The others, amongst whom Cathy.

* * *

When I reached home and opened the door to the small apartment, I was nearly knocked over by the smell of booze. It hit me as soon as I set foot into the building, making me want to turn right back around in my tracks. The sweet-soury whiff was sickening and my eyes watered as I closed the hardboard door behind me. A soft click resounded as it fell shut, followed closely by the rushed pounding of feet on tiles that only halted upon reaching the kitchen.

Floating noiselessly beside the silhouette of my father, whose body hung limply over the small wooden dinner table, my heart fluttered like a butterfly's wings. I could feel the claustrophobia tighten its grip around my neck, and my eyes dilated in the dim orange illumination of the room. The blinds were clamped shut and the only natural light sneaked its way in through the narrow gap created by the door I had left ajar. The musty air made it difficult for me to breathe, yet my father seemed to have no such problem as he sucked in regular breaths, his chest heaving up and down steadily. A silver sliver of saliva had formed at the side of his mouth and started to pool beside his heavy head. The liquid shone like raindrops in the scarce light and his face resembled that of a child. Even so, the dose of alcohol in his blood was clearly too much to be that of anyone other than an adult's.

A growling snore pulled me from my thoughts, startling me out of my state of lightness. Staying here any longer would not do me any good, and neither would it for my father. I realized he had not bought any fresh groceries either, so not much cooking was to be done on my part.

I summoned my cell phone from my pocket and typed in Cathy's number without looking down at the screen, my fingers pressing the keys while something inside of me broke.

I'm coming over, I sent. *It's happened again.*

And that was that. I made one futile attempt to move my father into a better and more comfortable position, yet his body would not budge, bowed forward onto the table with his head between his arms. Too bad. I filled a large glass of water and set it down within his reach; far enough for it to not be pushed over in his sleep yet close enough for it to be easily accessible upon his waking.

Then I turned my back on the scene and left the house in search of Cathy, who would console me and ease the puncturing wounds of shame and discomfort with her velvety words and gentle touch.

The sky gradually darkened, the clouds turning a filthy gray of dirty snow. I shot my way to Cathy's house, only one street removed, like a hot, shaky-legged rocket and arrived with wet streams of wire pressed onto my face. My weak fist only just touched the wood when the door was opened and I was guided in, led to her room like a lost sheep being herded back to the flock. No words were spoken until we had both sat down on her bed and my tears had dried on my cheeks.

Cathy was the one to break the silence, and when she did, she filled the room with comfort. She was in charge of the situation, which is exactly what I needed to be put at ease. When she allowed me to speak, my response vanished and my voice died away. Cathy took no note of my struggle and talked right through my failing words, forcing me to remain mute and take in her declarations like soft balls of cotton winning over the harsh thorny surface of my thoughts.

One spike still managed to prick through, however, when the following words appeared in the air: "The party I told you about earlier? Well, I understand if you won't, but I'm still going out." And as if to show the integrity of her intent she floated to her large bedroom mirror, leaving me alone on the bed. She pouted her lips to apply a shiny gloss, and, when I remained mute, shot back an expectant glance. Did she really assume I would come along? Did I at all look like I was in the mood for such a thing?

"Well, yeah. That's okay I guess. I'll just be going home," I managed, and in that instant Cathy's face both lifted and dropped. That wasn't the answer she'd expected from me.

She shook it off as if it was nothing. "Well, you should really get going because I need to get ready." She brushed her way past me, her perfume lingering in the air behind her. I knew it was way too early for her to be going anywhere, even if our chatter had taken up well over an hour, but once an idea was planted into her head there was no way she'd let it go. Within moments I found myself on her front porch without as much as a wish of good luck. But I had received all that I needed. I walked comfortably back home, making a little detour as the charcoaling sky surrounded me.

When I twisted my key in the lock at the strike of seven, my heart had been genuinely put at ease and my mind at rest.

I made my way to the kitchen, where I found my father sitting erect at the table, staring into space. The blinds had been brought up to allow the faint evening light to hang loosely in the room.

"Hey Chrissy." He carefully measured his words as they left his mouth. "I don't have any dinner or anything." It was the first thing he uttered while his guilty eyes found mine. I held up my hands in a way of response, revealing two plastic bags that I dangled in front of him.

"I passed by McDonald's on my way," I said as I sat down across from him. We ate our meals in silence.

CHAPTER TWO

Exactly one week passed before the next incident. On that particular day, a Wednesday, my morning classes passed by as if time had been sped up. The two-hour period it took for the bell to announce break seemed to have been programmed over an hour too early, but who was I to complain about that?

As Cathy had not said a word to me that morning and was now lollygagging with a group of boys and several girls, I decided to look for Marc. I found him near my locker, leaning against the cold turquoise metal while he ate a cream-cheese bagel from the cafeteria downstairs. His thumb flew rapidly over the keys of his phone as he absentmindedly took a bite of his snack.

My face automatically brightened at the sight of him, a smile coming over my lips instantly. He looked up from his phone and beamed at me. We embraced, and his rough skin against my own felt cozy and yearned for. We did not speak a word, feeling comfortable just being in each other's company. He motioned for me to have some of his bagel, as we always shared, and I accepted it willingly.

As the warm pastry slid down my throat, my gaze remained on his face, lingering on his slim nose and blue, twinkling eyes, like stars in the night sky. I sighed. He was the best boyfriend I could have wished for, the first boy I had ever opened up to and let into my life. Somehow, it all felt right, even if the other kids often walked by making those childish kissing sounds and other such immature gestures. They just needed something to busy their minds with and would pounce on any opportunity to make anyone and everyone feel uncomfortable. Marc, however, was different. Being two years older than me, he was more mature than all the other boys in my grade. He was a faithful lover, ready to get more physical in showing that love, but only if I was ready for it too. I wasn't, not yet, and he accepted this without protest.

I leaned in to kiss him, our lips joining like the swift brush of a butterfly's wings. My mouth tingled, and I smiled at him before turning my attention to my phone, which I quickly checked before the bell announced the start of my next lesson. The screen displayed one unread message.

Could you please pick up some groceries for tonight?

Issues at work.

Thanks. Dad.

Yeah, right, I thought. Issues at work. More like issues at the bar. If I were indeed to achieve my status of lawyer once upon a dream, how was I ever supposed to pay my college fees if he lost this job as well? I sighed as I swung my bag over my shoulder, took several books from my locker, and slammed the metal door shut behind me.

After break, I had history with Mrs. Ratpied. Routinely, I sat next to Cathy, with whom I had nearly all my classes.

The fading sound of the bell still echoed through the halls when Mrs. Ratpied passed out the tests we had taken during Friday's lesson. While Cathy animatedly went on about this guy that had moved in next door to her several days earlier, my mind was focused on a single thing. My test result.

I had gone a week without sleep to memorize all this information about the French Revolution. I had stayed at my aunt's house for the week, and she had continually stirred me up about going to bed and not using up all my energy, about needing to get sleep and it being the best preparation, yet I had ignored her advice and assiduously remained at my desk until the strike of midnight had long passed. I was sure my marks would reflect this, certain that the test would boost my already-high grade, yet when Mrs. Ratpied returned my sheet to me and I discerned the bold red-lettered F printed at the top, my self-esteem dropped to my toes. A small, circled note was included to the right of the looming letter: *Meet me after class.* Ashamed, I hid the paper in my desk, trying to conceal my disappointment in front of the others.

Someone in the back row yelled out that he had gotten a D, his friend retorted that he did too, and they high-fived at each other's failing grades as though it was a major accomplishment. A tear slid down my cheek and I angrily rubbed it off with my fist. I wouldn't cry. Not in front of the whole class. Not in front of *anyone*.

As if aware of my unsatisfactory results, Cathy sneered at me, her eyes turning to cold stone under her frowning brows and her pretty face turning bleak.

Throughout the remainder of the class I could not help but let my gaze wander out of the window toward the dark blue sky, where threatening gray clouds had accumulated to foreshadow the turbulent storm that was to come. I heard a distant rumble slowly gaining strength. The whole situation was simply beyond my comprehension.

When the bell eventually rang to release the class, I stayed behind as instructed. The students had only just dispersed into the hallway when Mrs. Ratpied came up to me and sternly inquired for my test, her eyes not their usual warm brown color. Momentarily, they seemed cold and hard and black, two frozen black marbles staring at me as if I were a dog that did not obey command. Except I had obeyed command.

Without hesitation, I took out the sheet from my desk. I was on the verge of asking her why she had given me such a grade – it really couldn't be possible, maybe she had given me someone else's test? – when she put up her hand, forbidding me to speak. I had seen her do this before, but never had I expected to be given the same treatment. I felt insulted but unable to object, too flabbergasted by the events that all suddenly appeared out of my control.

"Ms. Jacobs," – the fact that she used my last name gave me chills – "I believe you know why you are here." I abruptly shook my head to show her I had not even an inkling of what she was talking about. My light-brown hair waved around fervently.

Mrs. Ratpied frowned, and a vein swelled up at the center of her forehead. I had seen her this furious only once before, when she had told Arthur to go see the Principal after having written vulgar notes on the inside of the desks. Rather than do as he was told, he had refused to budge and his parents had to be called. It was quite a serious conflict, but this time things were different. This time it was *me* who was the cause of her irritation, though I still could not grasp why.

Mrs. Ratpied turned around to face the whiteboard – a sign of frustration as well as a method to prevent herself from doing something reckless in the name of anger – and that's when I noticed I wasn't alone in the room.

"Don't tell on me," Cathy whispered from beside me. She moved her hand horizontally across her throat as if to hint at severe consequences.

Don't tell on her? What was I supposed to tell? What was she even talking about? How could I tell anything if I had no clue what was going on?

Suddenly it dawned on me. If I had been in a comic strip, this would have been the moment a light bulb illuminated above my head, yet it now shone so brightly it cracked and the glass shattered on the floor around me. Cathy had copied my test! That's why I'd gotten a zero – the zero-tolerance cheating policy! She had copied my work before, yet it had never been detected by any of the other teachers. In fact, she had never really looked at anything but my homework. Or had she?

My breath quivered as reality doomed over my racing mind. In case of plagiarism, no matter the previously achieved score, the grade of that specific assignment was automatically brought down to a zero. And this after I had bent over backwards to cram all the material into my head! Cathy had asked me to keep quiet, but would that even be fair? She was the one to have cheated, so why should *I* have to live with the consequences? I would degrade myself and lower my grade and status solely to gain her friendship and approval. How could she even ask this of me?

My entire week of sleeplessness and non-stop studying was instantly reduced to the daunting F on the sheet in front of me. My life seemed to revolve around it; my vision blurred except for that bold red letter. My stomach twisted into a knot.

Mrs. Ratpied turned around, a shadow falling over her features as she flatly announced what I had desperately hoped wasn't true. Cathy and I would both get a zero for plagiarism, and if it ever happened again, we would be sent to the Principal and a note would be made of it. A note – *on the permanent record.*

"I do have one more question before you are dismissed," she continued matter-of-factly. "I would like to know whether one of you copied from the other, or whether you both agreed on... cheating?" She said the word like it was dirty, which I fully agreed it was. I just about opened my mouth to tell her the true story, I genuinely did. It was my chance to tell her I had done nothing wrong, that I hadn't even as much as noticed Cathy's glaring eye on my paper. Certainly Cathy would understand.

"I – "

"I'm sorry," Cathy interrupted. "*We* are sorry. We were not prepared and agreed to do this together, but we will never do it again. I swear."

I was completely baffled. My last chance shattered in front of my eyes; I felt helpless watching my last opportunity fly by right there, right then, without being able to reach out to it. I could no longer mend the pieces.

"What about you, Christina?" Mrs. Ratpied inquired. "Are you not sorry?"

I could feel Cathy's glare burning holes into my flesh. I found my voice and murmured that I was sorry too, after which I was forced to repeat it "like I meant it."

When Mrs. Ratpied dismissed us after what seemed like an eternity of humiliation, I bolted straight to the bathroom stalls, reaching the toilet bowl just in time for the sour mess to rise up in my throat. A wave of vomit caused my shoulders and upper body to tremble uncontrollably. I could not prevent the tears from running freely from my eyes as another wave of sour liquid rose. My stomach seemed to turn inside out, but there was nothing left inside of me. Nothing but emptiness. Nothing but shame.

I collapsed onto the floor of the bathroom stall and wiped the mess of tears and spit from my face with a paper towel, flushing everything down. I tried to compose myself but knew it was no use. I attempted to smile as if nothing had happened, but as soon as I opened the bathroom door the smirk was ripped from my lips. My heart jumped, after which it seemed to come to a halt completely. The air left my body as I jilted in surprise. In front of me, standing unmoving and poised, was Cathy. I forbade myself to cry.

"Oh, Dear, are you okay?" she said in a honey-sweet voice as she took a step forward to embrace me. I couldn't defend myself from her venomous friendliness, yet my mind was racing.

Was I okay? Did she have eyes in that flawless face of hers? Did she not notice my sheer misery? The sobbing recommenced, I was unable to stop it, and Cathy pushed me an arm-length away. I despised the irony of it all: her clothes could not get dirty.

"Darling, don't cry. You'll ruin your face. You have an entire free period ahead of you to compose yourself, but you don't really need an hour for that now, do you? Honestly, don't act like the world is coming to an end. It's just *one* test. Only one." I couldn't believe she was trying to calm me down like that. Firstly, she had copied from me more than once before. Furthermore, I had just gotten a *zero* on a major *test*. This would bring my grade down for the rest of the semester! I had just lied for her and so gotten myself into trouble, and I'd done it without protest. I'd done it simply because she had expected it of me. My hands shook and I could feel myself lose control, fighting against it but losing the battle. I knew I'd forgive her – I always did – yet the words flowing from her lips made me lose my composure completely.

I struggled free from her grasp and slipped past her through the bathroom exit. I could hear her voice trailing behind me, cursing at me for disregarding her, yet I blocked it out. I no longer cared about who saw my tear-stained face; the only thing that mattered was to break away from her before I would burst out in rage.

Yes, I'd always done everything to meet her expectations – I'd done her homework, let her copy, gone to all the places she wanted to go to and hung out with all the people she wanted to hang out with. But there was one thing nobody could ask of me, and that was to abandon my studies and degrade myself in the way I had just been degraded. How could I ever make my dreams come true if I had no goals to get me there, no grades to back me up? Somehow, I felt stronger than ever before as I strode toward my locker, not once looking back until I had gathered my supplies. To my surprise, Cathy had not followed me.

Systematically, I got out my agenda, my copy of *A Midsummer Night's Dream*, my pencil case and my binder, after which I made my way to English class. Before entering, however, I made a brief stop by the history room.

Mrs. Ratpied was busily typing away at her computer, her back turned toward the open door. The only audible sound seemed to be the hitting of the keys and the hush as I entered, the noises of the students' chatter in the hallway having suddenly died away from my perception. I closed the door behind me, but not before my eyes crossed Cathy's. She stood outside like a statue, staring into the room and keeping my gaze for longer than was comfortable. She would never forgive me.

With a quivering sigh I managed to pull myself away, and I approached Mrs. Ratpied through what somehow seemed to be so much further than the few meters the classroom consisted of.

Mrs. Ratpied looked up from the screen, her reading glasses perched low on her nose and her gaze stern. I shivered. Now was the time of truth. The time for me to prove myself.

"I... I'm sorry for what happened earlier."

Mrs. Ratpied remained an unmoving stone, not speaking nor moving – not even blinking.

"It... it won't happen again," was all I managed to utter, and I rushed out of the room and into the English class without turning back, my heart pounding in my chest and my nails digging into the flesh of my palms.

Cathy was already there, and so were several other classmates. I could feel their eyes piercing into my body, cutting into it like a hundred tiny needles, and intuitively I knew that word had passed quickly. It had sparked like a forest fire, and they were all tuned in already.

Instead of taking my usual seat next to Cathy, I passed by her without making eye contact. I wanted to go sit in the back where I would not be confronted by her, but my foot got caught and I tripped, my books and papers falling to the floor in front of me. I could only just hold onto a desk, thereby avoiding an embarrassing crash alongside my goods. My cheeks glowed hot pink. I rapidly picked up my belongings and glanced behind me to see what had caused my fall. Returning my stare was Arthur, who gave me a mischievous grin while returning his backpack to its original location underneath his desk.

I would not let him spoil it for me, however, and I wasted no time on him as I turned around, only to find Tanya standing in front of me, legs spread out wide and arms crossed over her chest. I had expected Arthur to take sides with Cathy – he was always in for trouble – but for Tanya to turn against me felt like a punch in the gut. When she had first arrived at Yarborough High, I had been the one to give her a tour. I had been the one to help her find her way and to guide her to all her classrooms. I had been the one there for her, forever open to her friendship in case she ever felt the need to speak her heart.

Defeated now, I turned back around and took my place beside Cathy, the only empty seat I *could* take, and she beamed at me as though nothing had happened. However, I knew her well enough to understand that the twinkle in her eye was not one of joy and renewed friendship. Revenge could be read in all the features of her face.

CHAPTER THREE

After school that day, I did something I would never have done before: I scrambled out the door at the first sound of the bell. I did not just walk, not even quick-walk, I *ran*, almost tripping over the untied lace of my right All Stars sneaker. Cathy's seemingly amiable face turned first surprised and then furious at my action, but there was no need for her to panic: her backup had already gathered outside the school building before I even got there.

My plan had been to avoid Cathy and get home as swiftly as possible, yet the crowd out in the courtyard prevented me from passing. It started off with only Tanya and Arthur, but soon a mob of curious others had arrived as well. There was a solid wall of students, and unless I could disappear into the vapor of my own fear there was no escaping them. The shouting and cheering overpowered the sounds of the commencing drizzle and the low rumbling of thunder in the distance.

In vain, I attempted to make my way through the mass, but I was pushed back relentlessly, forcefully, into the center of the circle by a wave of arms. Shouts slapped into me from all directions, and my legs grew weak underneath my body. I felt like they were no longer able to sustain my weight and could buckle beneath me any moment.

As if this was not humiliating enough, Cathy entered the circle like a graceful lion prepared to pounce, the crowd opening up to her and then closing behind her like I imagined the Red Sea did for Moses. With a determined stride she approached, looking me right in the eye with a hatred I had not thought possible for anyone to posses.

"Tell me, what did you say to Mrs. Ratpied? Did you tell on me?"

My lack of a response made her all the more convinced of my guilt.

"You *fucking* told on me. You deceiving *bitch*," she spat as Andrew grasped my arms forcefully from behind. I felt hands lock over my wrists like iron cuffs. Cathy snapped her fingers and Bob robbed me of my schoolbag, all too eager to get involved. He handed the bag to her, beaming at her all the while, and Cathy accepted it and opened it, pouring its contents onto the floor. Her sudden outburst of anger turned me to ice, and all I could do was stare as she ripped up papers and stomped on supplies. Notes. Tests. Textbooks. I could not have defended myself if I had wanted to, my feet curled into the floor with fear.

Cathy continued to ravage my stuff while I was unable to break free from my trance. Marc was nowhere to be seen.

I desperately twitched and turned like a fish on land, and, after what seemed like eons, I was finally released, dropped onto the floor like a lifeless lump. My bag had been dumped in the trashcan and Cathy had safely exited the circle of hate, yet not before I had noticed the glint in her eye – the small crystal sparkle that seemed to betray that she, too, would soon break. That she, too, felt betrayed. No longer sure of what to do, the crowd gradually dissolved and students returned to their occupations like nothing had happened. Like my life had not been torn into shreds before their very eyes.

In the corner of my vision I could see Maria rush by, our eyes crossing for only a moment but the unspoken message being stronger than any words could have been. *So it is not me this time*, they said – almost pleaded – before she disappeared from view.

With trembling hands I gathered my broken supplies and made my way back inside to my locker for my forgotten coat, only to find that Cathy had left behind a sign of her appreciation. A yellow sticky note with the bold words *you're too fat and ugly to hang out with me anyway* was stuck to the metal, and those words would forever be engraved in my memory. It was her handwriting; I knew she did it.

Blinded by a crimson haze of fear and shame, I ripped the note from my locker and threw it in the bin. I grasped for my coat and left, still trembling in fright, and I ran until I was certain nobody had followed me. Then I broke down to cry.

CHAPTER FOUR

Only upon arrival did I notice where I was – where my feet had guided me without my mind being aware of it. My sorrow had finally ceased to quiet sobs, and tears no longer blurred my vision. I looked around, observing the field of grass and the stream of brownish water that cut right through it. I was in The Garden. The rumble of thunder continued in the distance, and the dribbling rain washed away the thoughts of what had happened at school.

I lay down in the soft, rolling grass and pictured the walks I used to take here with my mother, next to the not-yet dirtied stream and through the tall undergrowth, picking flowers on my way. We'd stop from time to time to look at the fish or take a small rest, talking until the sky turned dark and the moon drew our figures in the water.

Though the pictures in my memory were warm and cozy, I found myself shivering. The piercing raindrops found their way through my clothes and reminded me of my current state. The horrific last hours.

I remembered my mother. My amazing mother. My dead mother.

* * *

That evening I arrived home late, having spent hours at The Garden without being fully aware of it. Memories of my mother had flooded my brain, and I could not pull myself away from them. I could not go home just yet. When I finally arrived, however, my father awaited me in the hallway, arms crossed over and legs spread out as though to take up the largest possible area.

"Where have you been, young lady? Did you take care of the groceries?" There was a dark undertone to his questions.

Instead of an instant excuse that would have been brought up by most teens of my age, I simply shrugged and walked on to my room, where I peeled my wet clothes from my body and changed into my snug pajamas. The fuzzy and soft cloth warmed me on the outside, yet on the inside I remained cold.

I went to bed immediately afterwards, staring at the ceiling until my mind became light and my thoughts drifted off. I felt myself being pulled away slowly, like a balloon rising up in the sky, away from the hurt and indignity. Though relieved from the pains of my day, my dreams carried me into a semi-conscious state that was not much better, as my night was haunted by screams and a terrible sting in my heart.

CHAPTER FIVE

"Good morning!" My dad said cheerfully. Too cheerfully. I was instantly on guard.

"'Morning," I mumbled in return, after which I poured myself a bowl of cereal, pulled back my chair with a screech, and sat down, my eyes not once leaving my father's countenance.

His face was long and narrow and his cheekbones stuck out from his recent loss of weight. He was a tall man, at least two heads above my own, yet his weight must have been only about 70 kilos.

Short stubbly hairs covered his chin and neck, and his eyes were red and puffy – whether from lack of sleep, alcohol or crying, I could not tell. His blue eyes caught mine, and I quickly cast down my glance. I could feel his gaze resting on me, his thick brows moving down over his eyes and his face contorting to a grimace. I had seen him do this too many times; the image was as vivid as if I were still looking right at him.

I ate my cereal in silence, listening to the crunch it made as I chewed slowly. My eyes remained on the bowl, yet I'm sure his eyes remained on me.

I heard the screeching of the chair as he left. I dumped the rest of my breakfast into the trash, brushed my teeth, hopped onto my bike and rode to school.

It was chilly outside, and the piercing wind snuck underneath my clothes and into my bones. I shivered and tightened the red scarf around my pale neck, pushing my way on to school, where I arrived ten minutes after my departure from home. Thankfully, I entered the warm building, the ceiling lights casting an orange glow and the radiator humming in heat. Most students had already dissipated into their classrooms, and a few exceptions sat in the common area, bent over their assignments and furiously writing away before the bell would pull them away from their work.

I strolled onward to my locker, threw in my scarf, my coat and backpack, and took out my planner, my pencil case and notes, which I had reorganized and strategically made to fit back into my bag before breakfast. I had put my notes in order and copied several that had become illegible; I had put the caps on my pens; and I had replaced my ripped agenda with a new, smaller one that I'd had on reserve.

Thus set for class, I walked on, seemingly casual while my eyes scanned every corner of the space around me. Not even the tiniest fleck of dirt was lost to my sight. I felt uncertain, but the only thing that could betray me was the shaking of my hands. The rest of me was still, composed.

I waved at Marc as I entered math, yet his eyes were focused on an invisible point inside his desk and my arrival went unnoticed. Cathy came to sit by me not much later, but not a word was exchanged between us. I spent the rest of my day quietly and pulled back, thankful for not having received the treatment I had gotten the day before. I silently expressed my gratitude to God, or whoever was in charge of minor people like me in this world, as I rode back home on my bike later that afternoon. I sighed with relief as I let the familiar scenes pass me by, my eyes scattered around while I took in the sweet smell of freshly cut grass. A spontaneous smile came over my lips as my hair floated behind me, playing with the wind. I felt like I was floating, like I was safe. Yet it was only of short duration.

As I turned into Caldon Street, I sensed an ominous presence. I looked around, but the narrow passage revealed nothing but shadows. The tall, dilapidated buildings and occasional stinking trash heap provided cover for any predator, and I decided to drive near the middle of the road for safety.

My mind raced. Maybe I was imagining it; maybe there was nothing going on at all and I was just making up scenarios in my head. I was driving myself insane. I'd always had a flowing imagination – what else could there possibly be?

I had almost reached the end of the narrow alley when I heard a cat shriek and jump away. I jilted in surprise, uttering a high yelp. I swayed dangerously before regaining control over my actions and redirecting my bicycle onto the street.

"It's just a cat, Christina," I murmured to myself. "Just a cat...."

I had only pedaled several more meters, however, when the eerie sense returned, stronger now than before. A current moved through my body as I imagined how small my presence must be, lost between the towering buildings on both sides. The world was engulfed in shadows as my heart was in fear. I picked up my pace, but it was already too late.

A shadow crossed my path. The air was ripped out of my lungs and my grip tightened on the bike's handles. Several other silhouettes followed, and I felt like I couldn't move, couldn't think, as I was encircled by the gang. I looked up and recognized Peter, Andrew, Bob, Arthur. Cathy. My heart stood still. My throat was sore and my breath left like sandpaper. My vision blurred, my bike came to a screeching halt, and I stepped off of it meekly; it was ripped from my hands almost instantly. In the corner of my eye I followed its path as it was shoved outside my reach.

"H... hey guys." I tried to sound calm, but I too had heard the crack in my voice. It had crept in like an unwanted visitor and simply would not leave.

Without saying a word the group approached, and I felt like a caged bird with a broken wing, unable to fly away. I'd never really suffered claustrophobia before, but momentarily I felt like my world was going to end, that I was locked in so tightly I might die.

"Yo 'Stina," said Bob casually, a smirk plastered on his face. "You've been bad. *Real* bad. You need to be punished...."

A hum went through the air, piercing it, splitting every atom of it. The hairs in my neck stood up, yet it was not from cold. Sweat rolled down my back and my eyes scanned the scene as though they had gone mad. I had not thought it physically possible, but the gang advanced upon me even further, shoulders mashing together and closing the sphere completely. I was definitely a trapped bird. A wounded bird. A damaged bird.

My eyes flashed around wildly as I took in the features of the bodies that encircled me, starting with Peter. He was of medium length and had yellowish hair – probably dyed – that stood up in tufts all around his head. He had thick eyebrows and a kind face, yet twisted into a grimace. His gray shirt was too large for him, and so were the pants that hung halfway down his butt. Faded jeans and sport shoes. Nikes.

Andrew, to his right, seemed like his polar opposite, being fairly short and plump. He had a stubbly chin and small brown glasses were perched low on his pig-like nose. He wore a red shirt and cut-off jeans. Similar sport shoes, yet of a different brand.

Bob –

My vision blurred with tears as a fist bore into my stomach. I screamed in agony. Around me I could hear laughs and shouts, encouragements to continue.

One, two, three. I had to keep my mind occupied. Had to think of something else, something that would cause me less pain than the torture they were putting me through.

Four, five, six. I needed to escape, yet how could I? I made a hesitant step forward and another fist seized toward me, hitting my ribs in a swift and powerful motion.

Seven, eight, nine. I curled up as red blotches clouded my vision. I couldn't see, couldn't react.

Ten, eleven, twelve. A blow to the side of my head and I lost my balance. I grasped around myself to prevent from falling, but there was no way to steady myself and my body hit the cold and moist pavement with a thud.

Thirteen, fourteen, fifteen. A kick on my back. Someone spat in my face.

Sixteen, seventeen, eighteen. A pressure on my near my temple.

Nineteen, twenty, twenty-one. Cathy's voice. *By the way, I slept with your boyfriend.*

Twenty-two, twenty-three, twenty-four. The world around me disappeared.

CHAPTER SIX

I awoke in bed, my father hanging over me, his face twisted and pale. The look of concern was unmistakable. I tried to smile in reassurance, yet my cheeks were too stiff to obey command.

"Hey... are you okay? Can you tell me what happened?" His voice was soft and clear, demanding in a tone that tolerates no resistance.

I shook my head as if to say, *no, I have no clear recollection*, but I knew this was not true. I knew perfectly well what had happened, yet what sort of further misery would the gang bring upon me if I told on them now? Would it not make matters worse than they already were? I decided to stay mute. I could always confess later.

"You don't remember what happened... *at all?*" he inquired in disbelief. I nodded. His eye twitched and his hand nervously stroked his brow. The last time I had seen him do that was at my mother's funeral, and I felt terrible for lying to him now. But what other option did I have? Tell on my classmates? Bring upon me more of their hatred? I couldn't do that.

Without even giving me a chance to speak, my father was at the door.

"Just call me if you need anything. I'll be in the living room."

I nodded. It occurred to me that I had not yet spoken a single word to him, so I quickly added an unconvincing "Sure. Thanks."

He left the room and closed the door in a hush, leaving me on my own. I wondered how long I had been there, in that bed, and how long my dad had been hovering over me, worried about my health. A damp cloth had been placed over my brow and a glass of water stood by the side of my bed.

It had gotten to him. The first thing that had gotten to him after my mother died.

Smiling, I fell into a dreamless sleep and did not wake up until I saw the morning lights take possession of the room.

*   *   *

Had I been sleeping an hour, a day? I had no idea, but I knew it was time to get up. My phone buzzed and I looked down at the screen. Two messages. I clicked Marc's name and my heart sank.

I don't think we should see each other anymore. I'm sorry.

It took me a moment to process the letters on the screen. They danced in front of my eyes as I tried to decipher them and make sense of them.

We shouldn't see each other anymore? Why would he say that? And why by text message? Did he no longer see me in the way I saw him?

Realization came over me like a dark cloud. So it was true, I thought. He had cheated on me with Cathy. That's what she'd said during the attack, hadn't she? *By the way, I slept with your boyfriend.*

In my mind's eye I could still envision us walking hand in hand, talking for hours until the sun went down. Not that we had been together for ages, but our romance seemed to have lasted a lifetime. Marc had not only been my lover, but also my best friend. How could I survive losing both of my support pillars at once; how could I manage without the ground underneath my painful feet?

I felt nauseous and downright stupid for never having had the faintest clue of what was going on. Why had he never told me? I thought that what we had was special, but apparently I couldn't have been more wrong.

My forehead nagged and my hand shook as I pressed the icon that popped open my next message. It was Cathy. Once again I was overpowered with confusion, and a blurry haze came over my eyes.

Nobody likes you. Go kill yourself.

Maybe she was right. Nobody would miss me.

I let her words sink in as I pondered them over inside my head. *Go kill yourself.*

With effort, I pushed my stiff body out of the creaking bed and washed my face in the bathroom.

It was swollen and bruised, my lip was busted and my right eye closed up. I looked awful, yet it in no way came close to what they had done to me on the inside.

Trying to keep the image off my mind, I left the bathroom and made my way down the stairs. I floated into the kitchen, where I expected to find my father. It was empty.

The instinct I had built up over the past year drove me right to the living room, where I indeed found him. A broken wineglass lay on the floor beside him, scarlet drops of glass scattered on the marble tiles. His body was strewn over the sofa, one arm on the backrest and the other hanging lifelessly off the couch and onto the floor. His legs were spread out on the cushions. His mouth was partly open, his eyes closed and his medium-short hair standing up on all sides as if an electric current had run through it.

I pulled my eyes from the scene and entered the kitchen, taking out a cloth, a brush, and dustpan from the cabinet underneath the sink. I cleaned up the mess my father had made, moving his body into a resting position and placing a blanket over him.

At a time like this I would usually leave the house in search of Cathy or Marc, where I'd be able to share my story and receive comfort in return. I would be solaced, helped to conquer my pain, yet I could not do so now. They were no longer there for me. I was alone.

Without saying a word or leaving a note, I left the silent house, returning only at dusk, by which time my father had recomposed himself, sitting at the dinner table as though nothing had happened.

This was getting all too familiar.

*　*　*

We ate in silence, eyes focused on our plates. The tension hung uncomfortably between us, yet I couldn't find the words to break it. Not painlessly.

After having helped himself to a second portion of pasta, my father finally took the initiative to speak. His glance still cast down on his meal, he mumbled, "I'm sorry, Christina. I swear I'll quit. I really will. It's just... difficult."

It seemed feigned, like a blank promise that would not be followed up upon.

"Dad..." I whispered in reply. "You've said this a million times before. You never do anything about it." In my head I added: Soon you'll lose even this shitty job you've managed to miraculously hold onto, and where will we be then?

At my words he looked up, his bottom lip jutted forward and quivering.

"I will, Chrissy. I promise."

But I'd heard it too often. My father overcoming his alcohol addiction – was it even possible after all this time? How could he promise to do something about it if he never truly intended to change?

This thought angered me, fury bubbling up in my body like lava in a volcano. First it came slowly, and then it spurted out all at once. "You *promise*?" I fired back sarcastically. "How often have I heard you say that exact same phrase in the past *year*?"

Pain cracked through my voice, seeping through the speech I had intended to sound strong. I knew my words would hurt him, but I also knew it was the only way to fight his addiction. He had tried it before, first confessing his wrongs, waiting for me to forgive him for them, promising me he would fix things. He would try to keep the promise for several days, after which the cycle would inevitably repeat itself. I'd seen it so many times I simply couldn't go through it again. It was too much. The last drop that caused the bucket to overflow, the volcano to erupt.

Tears now flowed down his face freely, a waterfall of misery, and I knew I had to continue what I had put into motion. I couldn't give in. My heart was gripped onto too tightly for comfort and my stomach twisted in sympathy, yet I stood up, shoved my chair aside, and fled to my room. I left my dad alone at the dinner table that night, weeping like a child, unleashing the pain he had tried to keep in but had been unable to fight.

I sat on the bed in my room, staring at the ceiling and the comforting light blue walls.

I'd barely finished my pasta at dinner, yet I felt disgusted with myself. Repulsed. I'd never before felt so useless, so uncertain and miserable. It was a different agony than even the death of my mother had been. It was an ongoing battle.

I pushed myself out of the bed and into the bathroom, dropping to my knees in front of the toilet bowl. My head felt like it would burst and I broke out in anxious sweat. The coolness of the tiles crept through my jeans and I shuddered as I stuck my fingers down my throat like I'd heard other people did. I gagged but was unable to throw up. I tried again, pushing my finger deeper down than before, but I was forced to pull back instinctively when my tongue pushed up toward the roof of my mouth. I felt a hot wave rise up in my stomach, but I simply could not go through with it. I wasn't tough enough. Not strong enough. Feeling more miserable now than before, I reentered my room with slumped shoulders. The weight of the food in my belly and the sight of the face that had looked back at me in the mirror disgusted me to the bone, yet fatigue took over and I fell onto my bed face-first, fully clothed, and did not wake up until the next morning.

CHAPTER SEVEN

It had been a week since the fight with my dad, and I hadn't spoken to him since. I still felt terrible about the pain I had caused him, the hurt I had clearly detected in his eyes, yet I knew it was right not to give in.

Having just stumbled out of bed, I now warily proceeded down the stairs, where I immediately noticed the uncomfortably spotless nature of the house. The usual pile of dirty dishes had been washed and the trash taken out. Not only this, but a plate of ready-made pancakes had been placed on an already-set table. I knew it was his restitution. The pile was *huge*, syrup leaking down the sides like sugar waterfalls. The exact thing I used to eat with my father whenever I felt down, whenever I dropped a Popsicle or fell off a swing when I was young. And now I hated him for it. For tempting me by putting it there, right in front of my hungry eyes. I couldn't eat it, couldn't even come near it.

I walked the few steps to the living room and looked into the two-meter tall mirror that was located there. I lifted up my shirt to inspect my belly – the bulge it seemed to form. The fat. I shook off the thought, pushed it away from my mind resolutely, and considered how to best deal with the situation at hand. Eat the pancakes? Certainly not. Throw them out? No.

I decided to leave them on the table as though I had forgotten to have breakfast altogether, had maybe gotten out of bed too late and rushed to school without having had a proper meal. My dad might buy that.

As I set my mind to this plan, I took my keys and cast one last glance at the person in the reflection. Doing so, my hand scraped the rough edge of the table and a fine cut formed on the soft flesh of my palm. Without paying any further attention to it, I took off, not even having noticed the note my dad had left for me on the table.

* * *

I arrived at school early, not having eaten and having raced the pedals off of my bike. The anxiety never seemed to cease, even though no serious bullying had taken place in the entire past week. I wondered what was worse: the bullying itself or the constant fear of it.

As I'd gotten used to doing, I stayed in the restroom until the first bell rang, after which I took out my supplies and left for class. When a hand unexpectedly fell upon my shoulder, my body froze in space. Not daring to turn around, I allowed my eyes to tiptoe sideways to the person that had appeared there.

Maria's face was gentle and shimmering. Her face was silent. My hand started to tremble and I could only just prevent myself from tearing up out of sheer relief of not having to endure another fight. Maria's hand squeezed ever so slightly and I granted her a failed attempt at a smile.

The moment lasted only a minute, if not less, but it seemed to last forever as I searched her face and she searched mine. We were one and the same, and we both knew it. Without a word having been spoken but with a million things having been said, she disappeared into a crowd of latecomers and I rushed to my respective class. My shoulder still tingled where her fingers had been.

I sat down in the back corner of the room by myself, no longer waving hello to Marc, who had broken contact with me since that awful day. In fact, no one spoke to me at all, and it was as though I didn't exist. I was of no importance.

The lesson went by at a snail's pace, minutes ticking by as though slowed down by some inexplicable force. The clock's hands seemed to be glued in place. When the bell finally rang and it was time for lunch, however, it did not come as a relief.

Making sure to be in the line of sight of a faculty member at all times, I hastened to the bathrooms and locked myself into a cubicle, my stomach growling, starving. I took out the sandwiches my dad had made for me the night before, attentively listening for any sound from the stalls around me. Nothing.

I took a bite of my full-grain bread with cheese and let the sticky morsel glide down my throat. It disgusted me, the way it lumped down my gullet. I took several more minute bites, deciding to leave it at that. I threw the rest of my lunch – a sandwich and a half – into the trash and went to the room of my next class. My stomach groaned in protest.

CHAPTER EIGHT

Several weeks passed and everything remained the same. Monotonously the same. Arriving at school, attending classes, spending breaks in the bathroom and trying hard to think of anything but the maddening hunger. The numbers on the scale steadily declined, my father unaware of any of it as he was never there anyway. When he was by chance home, I simply wore a large sweater or some oversized sweatpants and that was that.

Today, once again, I had not seen him home. Though manipulating his absences to my advantage, the lack of a father did hurt me inside. Sometimes I simply longed for someone to talk to, someone to ask me how my day was and make me laugh at trivial jokes. Someone to take care of me and pull me out of my misery.

Mechanically, I stepped into the shower and shut the sliding doors behind me. I turned on the water and let the hot stream pour down my fatigued body. My muscles were tense and my mind was elsewhere, yet the clattering drops on the porcelain solaced me, albeit shortly. I massaged my hands through my thinning hair, yet even this motion hardly kept my mind at bay. Though the situation had changed, my problem had remained. It was difficult to ever think of anything else at all. Yes, I'd lost weight – nearly ten kilos since I'd started this paranoia – yet I was still fat. The kilos disappeared, yet it was not visible anywhere on my body. I still looked huge. Dirty. Gross. I felt uncomfortable around mirrors and became increasingly uncomfortable around people as well. I spent a lot of time in my room, locked up and focused on not thinking about food. My life seemed to revolve around it.

After school each day, I read for hours on end. Reading took me into a different world, one where I could be anyone and where the scene around me was nothing like the gloomy environment I lived in. Everything was different, and for once I could lose myself in other people's problems rather than my own. Reading presented me with a place to be alone. A place to be someone else. Anyone else. Someone greater, smarter, prettier.

I squeezed a large amount of shampoo into my hands and rubbed it into my hair. What was my life still worth? What was I still living for?

Next to reading, I spent a great deal of time on schoolwork, being persuaded that the perfect grades would help me achieve the perfect me. I craved for people to notice me, to appreciate me and understand that I was not as bad a person as they might have imagined me to be. All I wanted was to be accepted, and so I worked on assignments all day and all night, only stopping to shop for the food I would not eat, clean up the mess I did not make, and try to get the sleep I would be all too anxious to embrace. On top of that, I oftentimes criticized myself in front of my bedroom mirror. It only reached from my waist to the top of my head, yet, if I stood on my toes and turned sideways, I could clearly inspect the shapes of my body. The rather flat chest, large belly. It's funny how I never noticed the prominently visible ribs, the bones sticking out at my hips. All I saw was the fat on my stomach, in my mind bulging over my pants like a piece of unsavory meat.

I turned off the shower and stepped out of the cabin, droplets of water covering my naked skin and my hair dripping onto the cold tiles. Absentmindedly, I pulled a towel from the stack and dried myself with it, wrapping it around my shoulders like a cloak. Condensation formed on the small bathroom mirror and I opened the window. Humming softly, I stepped into my bedroom.

My jeans and top were strewn over the bed where I'd left them, and I dropped my soft towel on the floor to get changed. Before reaching my bed, however, a craving stronger than myself pulled my gaze toward the mirror. With a guilty mind and eager eye, I watched my reflection as I approached, completely in trance.

Maybe Marc didn't find me attractive, I thought. Maybe it was me all along. My body. I took my breasts in both hands and pressed them together. It wasn't much, but at least that way it still looked like something. With a despairing sigh I let go, instead taking a piece of skin from my belly between my index and thumb and squeezing gently. If only this fat could be moved further up....

I turned sideways and critically examined myself. Hopeless, I thought. A stick would have more form, I dreaded. I neither had the chest so many other girls proudly paraded with nor the butt guys so longed to see on women. I was as flat as a ruler, apart from my stomach of course.

Without casting another glance at the creature in the reflection, I changed into my clothes and brushed my hair. Everything around me seemed to lose its value, slowly but surely fading into the background as other things took priority in my life.

I slammed the door shut behind me and flung myself onto my bed, where my laptop awaited me conveniently on the pillow. I opened up the device and the screen illuminated within seconds. Out of habit I opened the Internet browser, after which I clicked the colorful Google button for an hour or two of searching the amount of calories in bananas, kiwis, sandwiches, pasta. Searching models with bodies I wished to one day call my own.

After my search, I lay in bed and wept, my father at work or wherever else he was. He would leave home early and arrive home late, and I never saw much of him anymore. I was utterly alone, merely plunged further down into darkness. Not only was I ashamed and disgusted by myself and by the way I looked, I *despised* myself for it. More and more often I'd find myself inflicting pain upon my body, searching for sharp objects with which to cut into my flesh. It started off with the scraping of safety pins against my wrists, but I soon turned to other objects – needles, scissors, razors. It didn't remain at wrists either, as it soon evolved to include both hips and thighs as well. Especially hips and thighs. Strange as it may sound, I enjoyed the ease with which the soft skin was penetrated by the sharp razor....

Though clearly and willfully carrying out the actions, it somehow felt as though it wasn't me doing all of these things. It was as though I was merely an onlooker, experiencing it like it did not truly take place inside my own body. I felt detached, hardly even acknowledging the pain as I cut into the soft skin of my arms, hips and thighs. Deep scarlet lines oozed blood, which I put pressure on with a tissue to prevent from contaminating my clean bed sheets. The wounds remained, increased, deepened, and it gave me a strange sense of control. Line after line formed on my body, scars that would forever encompass my pain.

Although today I had managed almost an entire day without eating, I was miserable. I felt guilty about what I was doing, which only made me crave it more. I hated myself for cutting, and I cut myself for hating it.

I could already feel the piercing tingle on my skin when I snuck down the stairs to our small kitchen as I'd done countless times during the past couple weeks. I entered the area almost noiselessly, and the click of the hallway door falling shut behind me startled me. My hand shook as I pressed the switch and the bright light flickered on overhead. A stack of dirty plates had once again compiled in the sink, their shapes casting sinister shadows on the wall behind them. I took a step sideways, a sudden crackling noise extracting an apprehensive curse from my lips.

I looked down. It was just an empty chips bag. My rapid breathing gradually regained its regularity. Just an empty chips bag that had fallen off the counter. Just an empty bag. What had I expected? The place was cluttered with canned foods and junk, most of the fresh products having been disregarded since the start of that year. I pushed the plastic bag aside with my foot and bent slightly forward over the small drawer to the left of the sink. I opened it slowly, as though anticipating an unexpected creature to jump out any moment to startle me.

A sigh left my chest through my parted lips, and my right hand automatically grasped the cold metal at the far right, taking it out. I slammed the drawer shut and rushed back upstairs.

Back in my room, I unfolded my fingers from the object, the small vegetable knife shimmering in the limited sunlight that still entered my room through the partly opened window. The stainless steel glistened like menacing teeth, the handle falling comfortably into the palm of my hand. Without giving it another thought, I dropped onto my bed and rolled my skinny jeans down my legs and onto the floor. My finger traced a line down the pale skin of the side of my belly to the inside of my knee.

I clasped the knife tightly in my hand and pushed it deeply down into my skin, hot fluid rolling down my leg. Tears welled up in my eyes, yet I was unable to stop, my hands continuing their course without my brain having a say. A deep gash, another curvy line, more shapes. A tingle moved down my spine and tears now streamed freely down my cheeks and onto my naked skin, the salt entering my wounds. I winced, dropped the knife onto the linoleum floor, and rushed into the bathroom, where I pressed a fresh tissue against the open cut.

Blood stained the thin material almost immediately, and I pulled several more out of the box. My head felt light and fuzzy, filled with balls of cotton, and I sat down on the bathroom floor, my exposed skin shivering at the contact with the cold marble. I remained unmoving for several minutes, simply sitting there, blinking fervently to clear my vision.

When I was finally able to compose myself, and the bleeding had subsided, I warily got off the ground and stumbled into my bedroom, swaying dangerously.

I picked up the knife and cleaned up the mess I had made. Both proud and repulsed at the same time, I looked down at my body, at the freshly created scars. They were deep – deeper than I had ever cut before – and a dirty scab was already starting to form. *Freak*, it said. I had carved the words into my body without having been aware of what I had written. *Freak*.

And I was a freak. I had written it permanently on my flesh, and rightfully so.

I wrapped a bandage around my hips and slipped back into my jeans. The gashes stung, yet I deserved the pain. I deserved to be punished.

I never spoke to anyone about my self-harm, didn't even have anyone to speak to at all, and the struggle continued inside of me. When I actually saw my dad for the first time that week, he came up to me, his eyes red as though he had cried. He seemed open to talk to me, to be a listening ear if I'd so desired, yet I declined his services and so ruined my last chances of help. It appeared to be the first time in a long while that he noticed me, asking me how I felt while his eyes were glazed over with worry. I saw his all-too-familiar ticks of anxiety, the stroking of his eyebrow and twitching of his eye, his jumping gaze and hard line of a mouth.

"Is there anything I can do... anything you want to discuss?" he attempted one last time, but I did not respond, turning my back on him and marching into my room, locking the door behind me.

CHAPTER NINE

The chatter of the students in the hallway felt like the thundering stomps of feet in a stampede. My eardrums felt like they would burst and I wanted to clamp my hands over my head, to block out all sounds and sights. School was a drag, and I was glad to be making my way home at the end of a long day. The noise of the students exploded and I found myself in a chaos of arms and voices. I fought my way to my locker and then battled my way to the front entrance, where I could see a group of students had accumulated. But not just any students. Arthur was there, and so was Tanya.

Without slowing down my pace I walked straight up to the swinging doors, making a last-minute turn to the left into the bathroom stalls. Were they searching for me? Would they hurt me? How long would they stay, waiting like alligators prepared to pounce from underneath the smooth surface of the shallow water? The questions pressed down heavily upon my shoulders, threatening to snap me in half. Cold sweat accumulated on my forehead and my palms itched. Why were they doing this? Were they even coming after me at all, or was I just imagining things? My body felt like it was being slowly dragged into paranoia, the hot flames licking at my skin as I fought to break loose.

Suddenly I heard a movement – the ticking of feet – entering the restroom. Without a sound I locked the door to my stall and sat down on the toilet seat, pulling up my legs to my chest. I held in my breath to prevent giving myself away.

I had no idea how anyone could have seen me flee, but in case it was one of the gang that had just entered, she could under no circumstances find me here. Imagine what she would do if she'd discover I had taken refuge in such a cubicle? Locked in a small area and unable to get away?

My eyes skidded over the bare surface of the walls as I heard the sink run and the feet retreat into the stomping procession in the hallway. I eagerly sucked in breath. I was safe.

Even so, there was no guarantee the group was not outside, or remaining at the door for God knows how long. How long would they wait for me to come out anyway? How much was I worth to them?

My forehead felt like it was heating up and would soon burst right open, my thoughts being too wild and too cumbersome for me to hold onto. My eyes stung and my body felt cramped from the uncomfortable position, but I would not budge, would not make a noise, even when all others had faded.

An hour must have passed before I finally unfolded myself and hesitantly stuck my head around the corner of the stall. The school was as empty as children's playground upon the falling of evening. It seemed as though not a single soul was still present anymore, and my heavy feet echoed soft footsteps through the building as I made my way out. The strap of my bag cut into my shoulder and my curled toes were crushed with every step I took. I only allowed the heavy weight to be lifted, however, when I was sure I was indeed alone, and not a single corner of the courtyard had gone uninspected. My chest rose and fell and my sweaty palms were opened up to the fresh air.

Without wasting a moment, I fumbled my bike keys out of my pocket and propelled myself toward the rack beside the building. Except for the rusty model that must have stood there since the origins of the school itself, my bike was the only one still parked on the terrain. While my mind remained hazy with the wildest scenarios, I unlocked the thing and pulled it out of the metal frame. Only upon flinging my leg onto the saddle did I notice the bike would not go far. Both tires had been punctured to the rim and there was no way the bike could sustain me on my way home. I blindly flung it back into the support and ripped out the key. They must've been waiting for me, and the heavy threat hanging in the chilly air made my fingers tingle. They could still be near, waiting for the moment to appear and take central stage.

A scared prey, I rushed out of the cage that made up the school's fence, running until I had made my way home. The distance was long, but I took no note. I let the scenes rush by while my eyes were trained on the light I imagined ahead.

When I arrived, I bent double to regain my strengths, pressing my hands into the cool cement of the building. Catching my breath, my throat on fire and my feet pierced with hundreds of tiny needles of fatigue, I pulled myself from the wall and patted down my pockets. First the front, then the back. I then turned my bag inside out and went through the full range of motions yet a second time. Could it be possible?

My thoughts tumbled over each other as I envisioned my abandoned keychain lying somewhere along the vacant road, or maybe at the bottom of my near-empty locker, but there was no way I'd be going back. There was just no way.

CHAPTER TEN

I can no longer recall exactly what happened in the days that followed. Everything seemed to pass me by as though I was a ghost, floating outside of my own body and observing the events with a feeling of detachment. I had just passed an entire day at school, yet if asked I wouldn't remember any of it.

Fumbling the keys of my mom's old bicycle out of my pocket, I pushed open the large entrance door. As I left school and strolled into the courtyard, I heard a familiar voice shouting my name from behind. The hairs on my arms stood up and I desperately looked around, yet there was no place to hide. Discomfort crept upon me like darkness driving out the sun, and I continued my course as if the voice had never even reached me.

"Christina, wait. Come on, don't be unreasonable."

I yanked my bike out of the stall and maneuvered it into the street without once looking back.

Marc's voice trailed behind me, reaching me no matter how hard I tried to block it out.

"It was Cathy. I mean... Can you just listen for one moment?" With several brisk steps he was by my side, and he pulled me around by the shoulder to face him. My shocked eyes looked right into his familiar features as he continued, and I felt overwhelmed with emotions.

"I'm so sorry," he said, reading my countenance in a way no one else could have done. "I never meant to hurt you. You know that, don't you?"

I looked down at my shoes without saying a word.

"Don't you?" he repeated, yet to no avail. "God dammit, Christina, we won't get anywhere if you don't speak to me."

He put his hand underneath my chin and lifted my head up to face him. I didn't want him to, yet his touch felt so tender, so familiar, that I let him.

"I thought you knew...." He whispered, the strength having seeped out of his voice almost entirely. "Cathy... she... if I...she said that if she – or any of her friends – would see us together, they would bring something terrible upon you. I couldn't let that happen." He didn't seem the strong-willed boy I had fallen for. His once-daring eyes were now filled with melancholy.

"Dammit, Christina. I did this for you. For us. What are you doing to yourself?" His desperate glance slid over my body, making me conscious of all I did not have. His hand caressed my cheek and his stare pleaded for my attention. He moved his hand from my face and placed it on the small of my back, forcefully pulling me closer. His muscular body pressed against mine and I felt his breath in my neck. I weakly protested, but he didn't seem to care. Meekly I gave in, resting my head on his shoulder and relaxing my fists, only to have the shock fall upon me twice as hard.

In the corner of my vision I noticed a movement and my body tensed. Several students – I recognized Tanya, Arthur, and Bob instantly – entered the courtyard like predators advancing upon their prey.

I should have known it was a trap. Marc had brought them along, hadn't he? He had planned to catch me here... or was it all just one big coincidence?

My eyes filled with tears as I ripped myself from his embrace and jumped onto the bike. His desperate voice trailed behind me as I rode off into the distance with terror-struck yet furious steps. My fingers pried into the handlebars as though they were glued to it, my mind remaining with Marc as though nothing else mattered.

CHAPTER ELEVEN

Go kill yourself.

Everyone was against me, so was it really that bad a thing to consider? The tension inside my body caused an electrifying pain to shoot from above my brow down to my neck. Nobody would care. It would be a relief.

I observed myself in the bathroom mirror, my glance moving down over my naked and scarred body. Nobody would care, I was sure. Nobody.

My hands remained unnervingly still as I stooped down to pick up a bottle from the floor. I twisted off the cap with relative ease and poured the content onto the pile in the center of the room, where capsules and numerous other drugs of different sizes and colors already lay.

With clammy hands I attempted to scoop up the majority of the pills that were scattered there, and without another thought I tilted my head back and popped the handful into my mouth. The capsules got stuck in my throat and almost made me choke, and I gulped them down with tap water. It felt terrible.

Suddenly I remembered that I had not yet left a note for my father. An overpowering sense of guilt and concern drove me to stand up, yet the abrupt change of elevation made my head spin. The tension raced through my veins.

I tried to calm myself, but the scene danced in front of my eyes and I fell back, my arms waving around my body frantically. I grabbed ahold of the sink, pulling down my toiletries as I crashed to the ground. I began to cry and shake uncontrollably, my head leaning against the cold wall for an unknown stretch of time while I tried to pull myself back together. My breathing became increasingly rapid and I could feel my heart pounding in my chest. A nauseating sensation seemed to drown me, and my body shook in agony. My surroundings became blurred and the confusion made me break out in cold sweat. I could clearly envision Cathy in front of me, in the room with me, commending me on my common sense in undertaking this deed of self-destruction. The fact that I had finally put myself to it – finally had the guts. I could sense her leaning over me, whispering in my ear what a freak I was. Her expression changed and her features morphed into those of Marc. Marc....

I felt like I was gradually wrapped up in a warm blanket that shielded me away from the world. My vision disappeared completely and my senses seemed to be momentarily shut off.

As I lay motionless on the bathroom floor, the cold tiles pressed against my emaciated body and my face wet with fresh tears, I felt oddly floating. I moaned in agony, drool dripping from my parted lips as the pills numbed my limbs. Wrappers, boxes and bottles of medication were strewn all over the area. It would be a while before my dad would arrive and find me here.

He would understand, wouldn't he? At least he would no longer have *me* to worry about – no more trouble to take care of. It would be a relief maybe. Or would it not? What would he do if he saw me here on the floor when he returned after a day of hard work? Would he cry? Would I cause him even more pain than I had already brought upon him? Would he be unable to live with himself, without his wife and daughter, and take his own life as well?

I clearly had not thought it through, but it was too late now, wasn't it? The drugs were racing through my body, slowing me down and making me woozy. With the last of my energy, I crawled to the red phone on the glass table in the corner of the room, grasping around myself until I felt the object in my clutch. My weary brain raced as my numb fingers pressed the numbers, after which everything around me went black and I was engulfed by a vacuum of utter silence.

CHAPTER TWELVE

Beep! Beep! Beep! Beep!

I felt myself sinking away, yet I was vaguely aware of nurses rushing into the room, the scraping sound of machinery being moved, and the rustling of papers being searched. My brain registered shapes shifting in front of my blurred vision, voices mumbling hushed messages.

Beep! Beep! Beep! Beep!

I tried to breathe steadily, but the turmoil in my head wouldn't cooperate with my need for oxygen.

If I must die now, so be it.

One last time I strove to get my head above water, to scream for help, but the current was too strong. My efforts grew weaker as the strength drained out of me, and my fatigued muscles screamed for me to stop fighting. But I couldn't. I could never stop fighting, never give up without having given all I've got. Yet I was so tired....

There was a pressure on my chest and I suddenly became aware of my senses – the prickling needles in my arms and the pungent smell of disinfectant in the air. I gradually became conscious of my surroundings, though all was but a blur and I was unsure of where I was and why. Warily, I opened my eyes. Through a veil I unraveled the world around me: the pale white walls and the metal furniture. A marble sink, a small table, a chair. A person on the chair.

It was my father. He pressed my hand tightly in his.

Seeing my movements, he could no longer hold back tears, and I realized that he would never have survived losing me. I stroked my fingers over his, as though in an embrace that was physically impossible. We cried silently, shaking off the dread that had hung over our shoulders since the day that forever changed our lives.

I understood that my mother would never come back, but I now regained the confidence that my father would be there when I needed him most. He was here now.

He pulled back his hand from my reach, and I looked up at him. I hadn't looked at him for a long time. His hair had grayed and his face was decorated with deep wrinkles. He looked much older than I'd imagined him to be. He stared right back into my eyes, and I felt a connection we never had before, a current that pulled us together, telling me that my grief was also his.

In the silence of that room, more words were spoken between us than ever before. And even when he cut into the quiet with whispered words of comfort, they fell onto my shoulders like gentle pats of encouragement. He cared about me, and it was written all over his face.

Without leaving my gaze he said, strongly and determinedly, "I haven't had a drink since we fought those weeks ago. Actually, I've been seeing someone about my problem every day for the past six weeks."

And I could see that he meant it. He was fighting his addiction, and he was doing it for me. For us.

"I... I don't know what I would have done without you...." He mumbled, and once again he broke down.

There was still a long way to go, but we could manage it together. We both cried, clamping onto each other like there was no tomorrow. But tomorrow would come, and when it did, we would conquer it together. I knew we would.

PART TWO

Never let a stumble in the road be the end of your journey - Unknown

CHAPTER THIRTEEN

Cathy never came to visit me in the hospital. Not once. She did not even do as much as ask me about my whereabouts, possibly in the belief that I had moved away. Maybe she was ashamed. Maybe she no longer cared. But then again, neither did Marc.

Though tired as hell and terribly bored, unable to leave my bed, I could not sleep. The continuous beeps and buzzes, the traffic outside, the moving of objects and rolling of carts all prevented me from dozing off. The broken blinds and bright white hospital lighting seemed to mock me, and the screaming of babies and shouting of nurses all coerced me away from rest. Sometimes I simply wanted to pull the infusions out from my arms and run away from it all, to leave the hospital miles and miles behind me, but the clutter of nurses outside my room would prevent me from fleeing far.

So instead, I simply lay there, sometimes reading, sometimes staring into space. My eyes would scan the small crack in the plaster of the sheetrock as they had done a thousand times over the past three days. I was imprisoned, unable to enjoy even the most basic liberties of everyday life.

I swung my legs sideways out of the bed, careful not to disturb any of the machinery, and tapped my long fingernails on the large window to the left of my bed. The sound awoke the baby who was sleeping in the next room underneath the glass, and the girl started to air her discontent as a stout red-haired nurse entered the area.

The fat nurse ignored the noise and waited for me to speak, placing her hands on her meaty hips and tilting her head slightly. Behind her, a lamp flickered on and off, but she seemed unaware of any of the chaos around her. Her brows were curved down over her beady eyes, and her lips formed a hard line. She looked like she didn't really want to be there, but she gave me a sheepish smile nonetheless. I smiled back politely.

Her blue eyes examined my face skeptically, and she moved her weight to her right leg, shaking her hips awkwardly. Still, she remained silent. A rare contrast to the scene all around.

"I... uh... you know." I started, but the nurse did not take my hint. "You know...."

Her unimpressed face turned even bleaker, yet she nodded and shuffled to the back of the white-walled room. She bent down to pick up the small bucket-like pan and brought it to me in a slow and slurred movement. She handed me a roll of toilet paper, yet didn't grant me a moment of privacy as I relieved myself and then rapidly pulled my light blue pajama pants back up. She left the room with the same waggle with which she had entered, and before having uttered a single word she had disappeared. The door was left ajar and the baby on the other side of the thin wall did not once stop bawling. I felt exhausted.

Without wasting another thought on the noise around me, I thrust my head back into the soft feather pillow and was carried away into a dreamless sleep, a suffocating sleep of emptiness and complete oblivion.

When I eventually opened my eyes, I opened them to find a woman in her late thirties standing at the foot end of my bed. She had medium-long blonde hair, unwashed, that she wore in a ponytail at the back of her head. Her face was smooth yet shimmering of grease, and her blue eyes seemed to be placed too closely together. Her small nose was a button, and her chin seemed disproportionately large in comparison to the rest of her face. Still, she possessed a strange and unique beauty that was clearly conveyed in her confident stare and straight back.

Abruptly, she turned to face me, reaching out her bony hand for me to shake. I hesitantly offered her mine, and she squeezed it tightly while hurling it up and down. Her blue eyes sought mine, yet I looked down at my lap.

"I'm Dr. Paula," she introduced herself. "I'll be your therapist. We will be working together closely in the next period of time."

I pressed my lips together tightly. A therapist? For me? Who had come up with such an idea? I didn't need a therapist.

"I... I'm Christina," I muttered. "Do I... uh... is it really necessary for me to have a shrink?"

"A therapist," Dr. Paula corrected, "is absolutely vital when dealing with Anorexia Nervosa, which you have been diagnosed with."

Her flower-print top turned sickly green under the hospital glow, and it hung loosely over her rather meager body. Her jeans looked worn and faded, yet her face was kind and dreamy as she gazed down at me in the bed.

"Anorexia?" I exclaimed. I tried to cross my arms over my chest rebelliously, yet the infusions made this simple action next to impossible. "I'm sorry to object, but I don't think I have an eating disorder."

She looked at me knowingly, as though she possessed information I could only guess at. A meek smile came over her thin lips.

"The first and most important thing for you to do is to acknowledge the problem." She said. "In no case will this be easy, but we won't get anywhere if we ignore the issue."

I raised my eyebrows. Nobody had to know I had a problem with eating, and, anyway, I did not have anorexia or anything. I could start eating again as soon as I felt the need to. As soon as I'd obtained that image I'd worked so hard to achieve....

"Well," Dr. Paula continued. Her voice softened as she made her way to the door. "I'll give you some time to process and come to terms with the situation. It is important for you to come to terms with your eating disorder before doing so in front of others. Just remember that we can't fix a problem when we don't acknowledge its existence."

Dr. Know-it-all turned her back on me and exited the room, leaving me to take in the information, the accusation, she had only just spat at me. Anorexia? Me?

* * *

A blonde nurse came into the room at around three o'clock on Thursday, and I was relieved to finally be detached from the machinery for my daily shower. The short-haired woman popped the electrodes that were attached to the Holter monitor from around my chest and unscrewed the liquid-injecting needles from both arms. Her cold hands brushed my skin, making me shudder.

I swung my legs off of the bedside in a smooth motion, and I pushed myself out of the bed in order to follow her to the room at the end of the hall. While sliding my feet into my slippers, however, bright flecks of color popped up in front of my eyes from the sudden change of elevation. I held on to my bed and the nurse was immediately at my side to keep me on my feet. My legs swayed as I blindly put a step forward, trying to hide my dizziness and keep up the facade that everything was fine. The nurse slowly and cautiously led me to the small bathroom, where she allowed me to awkwardly undress. She helped me peel the clothes off my body, as fairly little could be done with unbending limbs. The tops of the injection tubes were still stuck into the creases of my arms, and bending them would mean pushing the sharp points through the veins and causing God knows what sort of infection.

The nurse bent forward and her nametag rustled at the movement. She pulled my shirt over my head while I held up my hands, and I discerned the name 'Patricia Becsi' on the hard plastic identification piece. She pulled down my underwear and my cheeks went red with shame like they always did.

Patricia took no note of my discomfort, and without further ado she guided me into the of-mold-smelling shower, turning on the water and waiting for it to heat up. She then put the warm stream over my head and helped me wash, a ritual that I simply could not get used to.

After my shower and change into fresh clothes, something I prefer not to dwell on for too long, I was guided back to my small and impersonal cubicle, attached once again to the tubes and infusions I felt no need being pumped into my body. I felt comfortably clean, renewed even – a feeling that would soon fade away again.

The nurse, having finished with the infusions, pressed the electrodes to the skin around my left breast and laughed when several popped back up.

She added some more gel to the rubber ends and carefully pressed them on again. This time around, they stayed.

Patricia smiled at me before making her way to the other end of the room. Her chocolate-brown eyes remained professional, and I sighed for the fact that she had not laughed at my flat-chested body and awkward limbs.

She placed her hand on the doorknob as she looked at me one last time. "If you need anything, just call me." And then she was gone.

CHAPTER FOURTEEN

I woke up at seven o'clock the next morning to the sound of the crying baby girl. I sighed as I heaved myself upright in bed and rubbed the sleep out of my eyes. My hands were clammy and my face hot with fatigue, yet morning had come and there was no way to resume sleep. I leaned toward the bedside table on my right, from which I took my fifth book in the past four days. It seems I devoured books like I should have devoured food.

I'd only been reading for several minutes when one of the nurses noticed my awakening and came in to disturb me from my utopia.

"What would you like for breakfast?" She asked, and after a moment of thought I replied that a kiwi would suffice. She disappeared as soon as I had spoken and returned almost instantly with the fruit. She gave me one of the cut halves and a spoon, and she placed the other half on the bedside table. She swiftly retreated to the back of the room, where she remained as I slowly scooped up small mouthfuls of the kiwi and swallowed them down. When I had finished both pieces, she took the skin from me and gave me a pleading look. "Is there anything else you would like? A yoghurt maybe, or some bread?"

"No, thank you." I replied. "I'm really full."

Her face fell and she turned around. Only once did she look back over her shoulder, but I had already reopened my book and continued to block out everything around me.

Reading was the only way to really kill time here – the only way to escape. Within moments I was carried away into a different world....

A knock on the door brought me out of my concentration once again. I fumbled my bookmark between the pages and looked up at the newcomer. A smile instantly came over my lips when I discerned my father, and he leaped to my side in the blink of an eye. He engulfed me in a bear hug, yet released me quickly to examine my gaunt form.

"Hey, Chrissy." He seated himself on the side of my bed, which creaked under his weight. "How are you feeling? How's the eating going?"

I'd accepted my eating disorder by now, but for it to be discussed openly remained a taboo to the devil that still resided inside of me.

"Of course the eating is going fine," I chirped back with feigned excitement. "I'm eating everything they give me."

I left out the fact that the nurses only gave me as much as I asked them for, knowing I wouldn't even touch anything else they'd put in front of me.

My father's face brightened upon hearing this, and he opened up the black shoulder bag he had brought along with him. He took out the all-too-familiar in-red-shiny-plastic-wrapped chocolate bar. My heart sank.

"I brought you a little something for your great efforts, and since the eating is going better and all...." He seemed a bit unsure of himself, but he handed me the calorie-bomb nonetheless. His face shone as I hesitantly peeled off the wrapper.

"Uh... thanks...." I took a hesitant bite out of one of the chocolate fingers. "Want to share?

There's two, you know. And I've just had breakfast anyway."

My father gave me a warm smile. "Don't worry, Honey. They're all for you. Enjoy."

I smiled back at him, the corners of my mouth curling up in a non-convincing gesture of happiness. "Thanks."

My father's gaze remained trained on me as I took several more bites of the bar. The grin never once left his proud features.

"So... how is Miriam?" I tried to sound casual, smoothly shifting the attention to a different topic as if I was perfectly comfortable with eating an entire chocolate snack.

"Miriam...." My dad repeated, the name rolling off his lips as though he had rehearsed its pronunciation a thousand times before. "As I've told you, I haven't had any alcohol at all since our discussion back when you were still home. I haven't even come near it. It's all because of her professional help."

I smiled at him, truthfully this time, and my heart was filled with warmth at the thought of my father having finally broken with his addiction. The progress he was making had seemed so unthinkable only several weeks ago!

His fingers stroked my hand while his eyes journeyed out the small window above my head. There was a hazy look inside of them, and I knew something was up. I could feel it.

"Miriam...." My dad continued as I inauspiciously placed the half-eaten Kit Kat on the bedside table. "She's a great woman. She knows the right things to say and do, and her help has been absolutely essential in my healing process. It still is."

I lifted my water bottle from the floor beside my bed and twisted off the cap. I took several gulps before placing it back, yet the lump in my throat remained. Was there more than simple admiration in my father's tone? Did there lurk something deeper, more dangerous to venture toward? How could he even think of loving another woman after having known my mother? I balled my fists at the tension that had started to crop up in the pit of my stomach. How could he?

"Well, onto you now. Any exciting experiences overcome you here? Any cute male nurses in charge?"

I hesitantly smiled as my father, having seen my discomfort, changed the subject to easier grounds. We spent the rest of the hour discussing work and life inside the hospital, even playing a self-created game of 'guess who?'

I sat up in bed as straightly as I could and put my chin up into the air. "You have to acknowledge the problem. That is of utmost importance: acknowledging the issue in order to fix it." I burst out laughing.

"It's Dr. Paula!" My dad gasped in between hiccups of laughter. "Five versus four for me. I'm getting good at this game."

"It's not a game," I countered in the same posh and heavily-accented manner.

My father finished my statement. "It is the reality. And we should treat it as such."

Once again, he burst out laughing, but this time my own face remained disquietingly still.

I looked over my father's shoulder and pulled up my brows to raise his awareness of the newcomer, yet my father, stuck in a fit of laughter, did not notice my sign. My gaze was fixed on the entrance. When speaking of the devil....

"Visiting hour is over." Dr. Paula stated coldly from her position at the door. "I'm sorry, but I have to ask you to leave."

My father's eyes widened as he looked around. He then returned his glance to me, his cheeks red and his lips tightly held together to prevent another crack-up.

"Oops," he murmured, and he bent down to give me a quick kiss on the top of my head. I heard Dr. Paula's fingers rolling impatiently over the windowsill, and my dad picked up his bag and left obediently. Dr. Paula remained at the door, arms crossed over her chest and hair tied back in her usual ponytail.

"Well, Christina," she said as she moved out of her frozen trance and advanced upon me. "We've made some progress in the past couple days, certainly, but you do understand that there is a need for you to continue therapy after leaving the intensive care, don't you?"

I nodded, being more focused on the idea of leaving on Friday than anything else. Only one more day to go.... How I'd longed for this!

"As soon as you pick your life back up at home, you will need to come in every third day, and if everything goes well, this might soon turn into one day per week. If there are problems, or you do not manage to gain weight..."

"Yeah yeah," I interrupted. "I know. If I don't reach the goals, I will have to continue the process through the inpatient program. I get it."

The doctor's face brightened. "Well, I just came to wish you luck. I won't be here tomorrow and there will be no further therapy today. I'll expect you in my office, of which I have given your father all necessary information, on Monday at eight a.m. Don't let your weight disappoint me."

She winked knowingly and turned her back on me. Pausing momentarily before opening the door, she pointed her index at the remaining chocolate on the bedside table. "Don't forget to finish that," she said, and then she rushed out of the room to her next appointment.

* * *

April 2nd, 2009
Dear Diary,

I know I do not write very often – I've just checked, and it's actually been half a year since my last entry – but I believe I do not have much of a choice today. I just need to get some things off my chest.

After having spent a week of torture in the intensive department of the Semmelai hospital, I've finally been released. I have now been home for two days, during which my father has overloaded me with attention that I do not feel I either deserve or want. He has also overwhelmed me with all my favorite food and treats, which I've often rejected or inauspiciously fed to our neighbor's cat.

In the past two days, my father and I have had more fights and arguments than ever before in my life. All were about food and calories, and all ended in me breaking down and fleeing to my room. The lock must be wearing down from its frequent use these days.

I don't know what possesses me sometimes, but I can't stand being told what to do regarding my meals and portions. I just can't take it – it's like I'm constantly being stepped on the toes, unable to relax for a single moment. Can't my dad just keep his eyes on his own plate and leave me to deal with this on my own? Why does he have to be so nosy all the time?

I guess he's just worried, but I can't take any more of this. I thought I'd enjoy spending more time with him, but in reality it's only making me feel more and more frustrated.

On Monday Dr. Paula expects me for therapy, and though I've tried to convince Dad otherwise, he has told me I have to go. "It will do me good." Though I guess he might be right about this, the thought of the visit is making me so apprehensive I feel sick to the stomach. Since I've been home, I've not gained a single gram in accordance to our agreement. Then again, I've not lost any either, but I'm certain she will not be pleased. I'm incredibly anxious for her reaction.

Christina.

CHAPTER FIFTEEN

My dad sat down on the red fauteuil in the crowded waiting room while I weakly knocked my right knuckle against the wooden door. Its white-painted surface had started to peel, and stickers of butterflies and frogs, probably stuck on to make the little ones at ease, had begun to lose their shine. Beside the door, a metal plaque indicated the office to be that of Dr. Paula Peknica, but before I could read the text underneath, a voice startled me out of my daze.

"Come on in," the voice instructed. I pressed down the cold metal handle and stepped inside, arriving in a place I would not have expected to look anything like it did.

Instead of seeing the imagined neat office room, I arrived inside a messy area, one wall of which was covered with folders of different colors and sizes, rather chaotically mashed together. In the back of the room, an old humming computer was placed on a bureau scattered with papers and forms, and next to the PC a bulletin board was filled with scraps, notes and pictures. The room was cluttered with patient-made artworks. There were three couches in the center of the room, surrounding the rectangular glass table on which two cups of tea and several more folders had been placed. In the far-right corner of the room stood a large measuring scale with movable weights, directly in front of a full-length mirror. My fear for this corner intensified greater than my OCD's demand to tidy up the chaos around it.

"Please take a seat," Dr. Paula said from her comfortable sofa that was located opposite the entrance door. For a change, she wore her hair down. She was dressed in a knee-length beige skirt and a rather plain black top. Her tights were dark brown and checkered, and my eyes followed her thin frame up toward her face, which did not contain a speck of makeup. I wondered how she could feel comfortable in her own body without any of the guises I put up for myself.

I sat down in the seat perpendicular to that of the doctor, and Dr. Paula took out a paper and pen in order to start our session.

"So, how was your weekend?" she inquired. "Is there anything you'd like to share or discuss today?"

I shook my head. What kind of a question was that anyway? Wasn't it up to the therapist to decide upon the topic and then search the patient's brain for the answers? I had not expected to be questioned in such a way, and my mind raced as I sought for something to say.

"I don't have any specific topic to discuss, but my weekend was good. It was nice to be home."

She nodded, recording something on the paper in front of her. "Did you do anything special together? Was there anything in particular that you did that you missed when in the hospital?"

"Not really. I mean… I don't think so." Again, she nodded, penning some more notes onto the paper.

"Well then," she stood up from her seat, straightening the folds that had formed in her skirt. "Let's start off with a measurement of your weight."

When I remained unmoving she clapped her hands and urged me on. "Chop-chop. Take off your clothes and come to the scale over here. We don't have all day."

She made her way to the large machine, where she impatiently awaited me. I felt uncomfortable and exposed in front of her prying eyes, but if that was what was expected of me, what else could I do?

Having stripped off my security, I shuffled toward the intimidating machine that was to determine my future. I lifted up one foot, but Dr. Paula pushed me back, taking me by the shoulders and turning me around. She made me step onto the scale with my back to the weights. She also measured my height, after which I was told to get dressed again. I was relieved to put that layer of protection back on.

"Well," Dr. Paula announced, jotting down some new information. "According to my measurements, your current weight is 28.5

kilograms, and with a height of 1.60 meters, that makes a BMI of... 11.1."

She let the information sink in before continuing. I had known my weight to be low, and I'd checked often enough to know exactly how much it was, yet her speaking of the facts caused a shock to radiate through my body. I was proud of having reached this weight, yet at the same time I felt a different sensation, one of guilt and disgust, stir up in my body.

"A normal BMI lies somewhere between eighteen and twenty-five, and the proper weight of a sixteen-year old girl of your height should be between fifty to sixty kilos."

She showed me a chart that had been lying on the table in front of her and I nearly choked on a sip of the tea that had been nudged toward me. My eyes almost popped out of their sockets in shock. Fifty to sixty kilos? That would mean I'd need to double my current body weight, which would simply be insane!

"Seeing that your entire family is quite thin, however – and the fact that you've previously weighed no more than 40 kilos according to your earlier statements – this would not be a reasonable goal."

I let out a sigh of relief as I processed the information. No fifty to sixty kilos for me!

"I believe we should strive for the original 40 kilos first, and then we can go on from there."

"Go on from there?"

"Well, yes, of course," she explained. "You can't stay on the same weight forever. I think our ultimate goals should be between forty and fifty kilos, and even that would be quite generous of me."

"But..." I objected, "when do you envision me gaining all this weight? And *how*?" My voice went up a notch and my face turned red from the cropped-up tension. I couldn't do it. I really couldn't.

"I know you work hard in school," the therapist simply stated. "And you can apply the same principles in weight gaining. I know you can do it."

I gulped in a gust of air. "That's different –"

"No, it's not." She claimed. "And by Thursday, you should have made the 29 kilos, which is certainly not much to ask. I've had patients gain more in this time. Do you think you can do that?"

I nodded.

Dr. Paula stood up from her sofa and reached out her hand for me to shake. "Well then, let's do this. Could you bring in your dad for a moment please? I'd like to discuss the situation with him."

And with that, the therapy was over. I shook her hand and left the room, sending in my father for several minutes before going home.

In the car, my dad turned down the music and searched my face. I looked out of the window, but I could feel his stare and its underlying questions.

"That went pretty well, right?" I turned my head to face him.

"It seemed good to me," he contributed. "But how do *you* feel about it? About the weight and all."

"Oh... well, I think it's reasonable. I mean, I can't go on looking like *this*." I motioned at my body, seemingly lighthearted, and laughed at my own joke. My dad did not join in. Instead, he placed one hand on his brow and stroked it nervously in place.

"Chrissy... are you sure? Is it no problem for you? You know I'll be there to support you the entire time, right? I will always be there for you." And with these words, the conversation was ended. I turned to face the scene outside once again, pushing back the tears that threatened to disturb the peaceful atmosphere.

*   *   *

April 5th, 2009
Dear Diary,

Today is Wednesday, meaning that tomorrow I have to visit the doctor again. I have a strong urge to once again pen down my thoughts – an urge I've never had before.

Yesterday (with my kiwi breakfast!) I ate a slice of bread with Nutella. My dad made me. I was both proud of my achievement as well as completely devastated by it, and when I got to my room I cried for an hour. I just couldn't help it – it was stronger than myself. To break even for this sin I restricted my lunch portion, but in the evening I once again made an unexpected turn and took a small scoop of ice cream for desert, a treat I had not had for ages. My father was overjoyed by this initiative, and he was incredibly proud of me. So was I.

This morning, however, I was shocked to see that my weight has gone up to the desired 29 kilos. I should stop eating so much – I don't want it to be higher than it has to be.

At this moment my aunt and uncle are here. They said they wanted to see me, and they gave me a nice book as a present and motivation for my recovery, but I think the true reason they came was to see my father. You see, my father and his brother haven't really spoken for a long time, and I think it is about time they made up. Dad has been alcohol-free for a while, and I think this must have been the reason for the unannounced reunion.

Anyway, I hear feet coming up the stairs so I'll just close with this. I'm anxious for tomorrow.

Christina.

CHAPTER SIXTEEN

"Very well," Dr. Paula said as she took her seat. "I can see you have the willpower to get on top of this illness."

I smiled wryly at her as the numbers tumbled through my head. 29.2 kg. 200 grams too much.

Dr. Paula swung one leg over the other and folded her hands in her lap. "How do you feel about this weight? It's not much of a difference, but it's a start."

I looked her in the eye but could not find the words to respond. Instead, I shrugged, seemingly indifferent while the question marks piled up inside my head. I'd worked so hard to get my weight down and it had taken me months, and now it went up just like that? That wasn't fair. And why was this happening to *me*? There were loads of other skinny girls out there that should get their weight up, so why was I the one to have been found out, forced to once again revert to 'normal'? I realized it was only half a kilo, but it was half a kilo in the wrong direction.

Dr. Paula studied me as if to search my face for the answers. "You are very unreadable. Compared to my other patients, I mean. It would be beneficial if you would speak up a little. That way I can better treat you." But what was there to treat? What was there she wanted to change? Did she want to turn me back into the blubber monster I was before? No thank you....

Dr. Paula's gaze relaxed as she continued, unaware of the thoughts that were bouncing around in my head. "For our therapy today, is there anything you would like to discuss? Is there anything you would like to share?"

Again that dreaded question. Why did *I* have to come up with a topic of conversation? Wasn't that up to her – the paid professional?

I shook my head, aware that I had not said a word since my "good morning" ten minutes earlier. I did not feel the urge to open my mouth.

A vibration was born inside my stomach and I wished desperately that Dr. Paula would not hear its rumbling. I had not had much of a breakfast, and letting my stomach speak instead of me was not really the road I wanted to take. My fists tightened but relaxed again when Dr. Paula simply went on, my stomach screaming for her attention. Either she did not hear it or she chose to ignore it, but I think it must've been the latter. Either way, I was relieved it was not brought up and the therapy continued its usual course.

"As you have no pressing questions or concerns," she unclicked and then clicked her pen as she spoke, "let's start off talking about your life at home. You've been back for about a week, so how did you experience these days? Did you do anything fun you'd like to share?"

It seemed like Monday's therapy all over again. I knew I needed to speak up now, but each time my mind searched for the answers it reached an impassable wall.

I pulled my gaze loose from the suffocating eye contact we'd had and spoke softly: "Well, we've not done much. Mostly just stayed at home, played some board games, watched some movies. You see, my father doesn't really want me to do things that require energy because of the weight. Oh, and yesterday my aunt and uncle came for a visit, but they only stayed for about an hour or so...."

Dr. Paula nodded and jotted down some notes. I was finished with my recollections but she seemed to be expecting more. She looked at me, speechless, for at least a minute before she allowed her own voice to shake the tranquility in the room. It was awkward, uncomfortable, and I wondered if she experienced it the same way. Maybe she was trying to pull more information out of me, but my lips had already been sealed and locked silent. I had nothing more to contribute.

"Well that seems nice," Dr. Paula remarked, and I nodded. "Did you enjoy the visit? Was it fun?"

Again, I nodded.

"How was your mood over all? Let's say on a scale from one to ten, one being terrible and ten being absolutely ecstatic?"

I let the days flash back through my head and then blurted "eight" without giving it much thought. Eight seemed reasonable, didn't it? At least it did not seem like I was trying too hard.

Again, Dr. Paula made notes. How I wish I could look at her papers to see what kind of things she penned down constantly! Her gaze moved back up and reached my face. "An eight, you say? Why eight? Was there anything you did that did not go as you'd have liked?"

I thought for a moment about her question but it was hard to keep my concentration.

"Uh... I guess I chose eight because I felt quite good," I lied, "but at the same time I have to, of course, get used to just being back again. That's all."

"Were there any unpleasant thoughts you had upon being back at home?"

I shook my head, knowing that every time I had entered my bedroom I'd felt like I was short on oxygen, struggling to break free from the clamps that had held me prisoner for so long.

"Okay," Dr. Paula said lightly, lifting the heavy air. "That's enough. I can see you're a bit uncomfortable and I don't want to push you any further. We'll try again next time. For now, let's discuss your weight. Our next therapy will be in one week's time and I believe you can gain another 500 grams, if not more. What do you think?"

I nodded sheepishly. Another 500 grams. If not more. I folded my arms over my ribs and felt a strong urge to rock back and forth like a child. Only just being able to suppress it, I leaned into the soft cushion and then pushed myself back upright. 500 grams.

"Well, if that's sorted, I will see you next time. Please invite your father in for a moment and I'll be awaiting you here in one week."

I shook her hand without much willpower and she responded with a strong squeeze of her own. I called in my father and in no time we were on our way back home, not a single word hanging between us until we arrived and I requested to go to my room.

* * *

Being home seemed just about as bad as being in the hospital at times. At least that's what I thought when I was screaming so loudly I could feel my vocal cords quivering inside my throat, all to overpower my father's bellowing roar.

"Christina, get back down here." He would tolerate no disobedience. "Just an apple is no breakfast, and you know that well enough. Get back down here."

I blocked out his voice and continued my way up the stairs, stomping loudly merely to push his buttons more. "I told you, I'm not coming. I'm full, leave me alone!"

I heard my father's feet follow me up the stairs so I quickened my pace until I reached my room. There, I smacked the door shut and turned the lock, only to find that the key would no longer budge. He'd changed it; he didn't trust me.

My father knocked politely on the door, but my reply was all but polite. "Go away! Don't you dare come in."

The threat hung in the air like a guillotine, the blade ready to strike down if only the opening door would set it into motion. But the door remained shut.

"Chrissy, Honey," my father murmured through the wood. "Don't you want to get better? I can't just sit here all day and look on as you self-destruct. I just can't."

I pressed my hands into the door where I imagined he had planted his. My shoulders shook. My father's voice was filled with pain and helplessness, but how could I explain to him that I, too, felt helpless to the voice inside my head? At times I felt like I had as little control over the situation as anybody else, looking on as the girl that was me continued on her course of disintegration and demolition. I was powerless, having given up the strings to the man inside my head.

What was wrong with me? Why could I not just flip the switch and see all the brightness ahead if only I chose the correct path? Or rather, why could I see the correct path but not choose to tread upon it?

My right hand traced the surface of the smooth door as I turned my back to it, pressing my shoulder blades into it as I allowed myself to slide down onto the hard floor. Why did it all have to be so difficult? Why was there no manual telling me what was right and what was wrong – what I should and shouldn't do? Why couldn't it just be written out, step by step for me to follow without needing to question a thing?

"Chrissy, please. Can I come in?" My dad's voice was almost pleading now, yet still he refused to press the door handle without my consent. "Please...."

Without saying a word I pushed myself up from the floor and opened the door, coming eye to eye with my father. His large hands hung limply to his sides, and the edges his heavy eyes were pulled down toward the corners of his lips. He looked defeated, and there is no way to describe his features any differently than that.

I fell into his arms and he carried me down as if I was still his little girl, my head pressed into his neck as the stairs creaked underneath our joint body weight.

He seated me at the breakfast table, where we both had a ham sandwich. He with a loving and satisfied smile on his face, and I with a broken and trying-to-hide-it one on mine. After the meal my father managed a silent "thank you" through his tight line of a mouth, and I made my way to my room for the second time that day.

It was the first time I ever managed to throw up, but I am proud to say that it was also the last.

CHAPTER SEVENTEEN

April 11ᵗʰ, 2009
Dear Diary,

I don't at all feel like writing, but I need to share with you that my weight has been deteriorating day by day. I am both proud and ashamed.

This morning my weight was, as my dad called it when he unexpectedly bolted in, 'disappointing,' so I guess I should really get eating more in order to make the extra 500 grams for Thursday. I can do it. I'll show Dr. Paula how strong-minded I can be.

Christina

CHAPTER EIGHTEEN

I pressed my lips tightly together as Dr. Paula fired the accusations at me. Each word she spat felt like a direct attack on my sanity.

"*You* were in control." She said. "I gave you my trust, and you simply abused it. Don't let the devil inside your head make the decisions, but choose to take control over your own actions. You have to see the full picture. Remember what I told you about seeing the entire forest rather than focusing on just one tree? That's exactly what you need to do."

I nodded, as I indeed remembered that. I needed to stay motivated, to envision my goals and the consequences of my actions. I knew it all, yet why was it so difficult to put it all into practice?

Dr. Paula continued, softer yet more sternly now. "I believe it would be better for you to continue an inpatient treatment. I didn't want to do this, but with a weight of 27.80 kilos you've lost over a kilo in the past week. You're two kilos from what you should have been by today. This is a dangerous trend I don't want to see continued, and if we don't stop it now, you will land in the intensive care again in no time – tube fed and powerless."

The thought of being force-fed with a tube through my nose made the hairs on my arms stand up. This is not what I had aimed for....

"I contacted your father on the phone yesterday to go over the what-if situations, and he stands by me in the hospitalization. What do you think about it?"

Momentarily anger bubbled up inside of me, but it immediately subsided to powerless surrender. "Well... uh... my father agreed?" – I couldn't imagine him doing this to me – "Then... uh... I'll try that I guess. It's not like I have a choice." I sighed.

"Listen," the doctor countered. "You always have a choice. It is ultimately up to you: do you want to get better or not? Would you like to be happy or would you prefer to continue your course more dead than alive?"

"Well, of course I want to be healthy." I protested, and I meant it. "But I can achieve that at home, can't I? There's no need for me to be *imprisoned* here to achieve the desired effect."

Dr. Paula's face grew thunder sky gray. "Well, apparently you can't. I gave you a chance, but it didn't work out. I honestly believe we should give this a try, seeing as you are currently still in a life-threatening situation and something has to happen immediately. As soon as your weight will start to go up, your mindset will automatically change alongside of it."

I nodded dejectedly, knowing I was powerless in the face of her decision. I was permitted to go home to get my goods, and the entire car ride back streams of betrayal slid down my cheeks. My father stolidly watched the traffic ahead, even when the accusations were fired around his head. He acted as though he was unaware of my pain, yet, upon looking up at him through my red swollen eyes, I could clearly see that he was broken too.

* * *

Upon arriving at the hospital with my bags, a nurse with blonde-dyed hair led me through a long hallway, where I was forced to say my goodbyes to my father while she unlocked the colossal entrance door.

"Take care," my dad whispered into my ear. "I know you can fight your way through this. I will come by every day, I promise." And with those words he was forced to leave me on my own.

As soon as I set foot into the corridor, my bags were checked and my vitamin pills, deodorant, and nail clipper were taken away from me. It was like going through customs at the airport, the destination being hell.

"We'll store your goods here," the nurse said, pointing to one of the drawers. "If you ever need any of it, tell one of us and we will supervise you during use. Also, we will give you your medication each morning after breakfast. You'll get to know the rest of the rules sooner or later."

Without wasting another word, she led me further through the hall of the child psychiatric ward. In several of the rooms I could hear talking, hysterical laughter, shouts, and I wondered how I would ever survive here. At the end of the hallway, I was shoved into a room on the right-hand side. My room.

"This will be your bed for the next period of time," the nurse explained, pointing to the last bed in the row of three. "Well, settle in."

"Thanks," I mumbled, but she was already gone. Hesitantly, I moved my bag onto the bed and started filling the small cabinet that supposedly was mine. Upon looking up, a boy and a girl, both between the ages of fifteen and seventeen, had appeared at the entrance to the room, yet the boy quickly left when I noticed him. The girl, her hollow stare focused upon me and her sunken cheeks forced into a smile, shuffled in, however, seating herself on the first bed and not once taking her eyes off of me. She wore black leggings through which her edgy knees were clearly visible, and her white shirt hung lifelessly over her bony shoulders. She waved at me, her stick arms swinging through the air awkwardly, and I looked down at my lap in misery. I didn't look like that. I didn't. This thought made me both relieved as well as ashamed. I blushed at my own twisted ideals, but I had somehow hoped I'd be skinnier than her. It felt like a defeat not to have made it further down than she had, but at the same time I knew it should have come as a relief.

Another girl walked in and smiled politely at me when she sat down on the second creaking bed. She had bright red hair, rather short and wavy, and she wore a much-too-large black Metallica shirt and skinny jeans.

"Hey, you're new here, aren't you? I'm Becky, and that's Sara. She doesn't speak English though. She's a bit weird."

I laughed at her bluntness when the blonde nurse returned with a form, her face predicting stormy weather.

"Your name is Christina Jacobs?" she barked.

I replied affirmative.

"You're sixteen?"

Again, I nodded.

"You take medication. Once a day?"

"Yes. But it's only vitamins…"

"You're here for Anorexia Nervosa?"

I looked around at my roommates to see their reaction. Though Sara was clearly paying attention,

Becky hardly registered what was going on or simply did not want to appear nosy.

"I... uh... yeah." I mumbled in reply, and the nurse disappeared as she had come. My cheeks were hot red, yet Becky took no note of it, acting as though the nurse had never even shown up at all. She stood up from her bed and advanced upon me, her face bright through the presence of a smile.

"If you want, I can introduce you to some of the others?" she offered, but I declined. I preferred to get my stuff in order and take it slowly.

She shrugged and walked toward the door, yet I stopped her with a question.

"If you don't mind my asking... why are you here actually?"

Becky stood still in her tracks. Without a change in neither the features of her face nor a single moment of hesitation, she blurted "Bulimia," after which she explained further what had driven her into her current state. She seemed at ease with the subject, as though she had fully accepted it and now regarded it as a simple life event.

"Well, you see, my parents thought it was getting out of hand, and so they decided to have me hospitalized. I'll be going home soon, though."

I was surprised at her straightforwardness and honesty, and both happy she would go home soon as well as disappointed she would be leaving me here to sort things out by myself. I know it sounds selfish, but how would I survive this hell all alone?

She left the room just as my phone vibrated in my pocket. I quickly took it out and unlocked it, after which I mechanically pressed the inbox button. Rather than the expected good-luck message from my dad, it was a message from Marc.

Why are you not in school? You've been missing so much. I'm worried about you. I hope we can make up.

Yours always, Marc.

My fingers flew rapidly over the keys as I typed my response. Before being able to send it out, however, a plump brown-haired and sullen-looking nurse came in and took the phone from my hands in a rough and brutal motion.

"No phones allowed," she growled, and she left without granting me another glance. How was I ever going to survive this hell?

*   *   *

"Lunchtime!" a hoarse female voice echoed through the halls. "Lunchtime! Everyone out of your rooms."

Muddled, I pushed myself out of the bed and into the hallway, closely followed by Sara, who had been staring aimlessly into space ever since the nurse had left.

I joined the group of people to the set of four tables at the left end of the hallway and took place in the seat next to Becky, which luckily was free. The blonde nurse set down sets of eating utensils for all patients while the brown-haired nurse scooped soup into the designated cups. The disgusting broth was soon placed in front of me, and I noiselessly scooped the thick sludge into my mouth. All of it, and without protest. I thought I might vomit any time.

"Lunch is usually made up of a soup and a main course," Becky whispered to me. "But the other meals are all fairly reasonable. Don't worry too much."

I smiled wryly as, immediately after having finished my soup, the main course was brought and a plate of cold mashed potatoes and stroganoff was placed in front of me. Though in no way coming near to my father's culinary abilities, I swallowed the food down and returned my plate to a nurse, who was struggling to get a nine-year old boy off of her. He was clamped onto her like a bloodsucking tic, trying to kiss her and tell her how much he loved her. At the same time he drooled all over the place, and the nurse appeared clearly uneasy with the situation. She tried to get him to sit down and eat his meal, but he refused to budge. She accepted my plate and placed it on the metal tray with the other empty plates, yet the drooling boy did not give her a break. He held onto her wrists and leaned forward to kiss her again, but the other nurse took hold of him and carried him off.

I pushed back my chair and stood up, intending to return to my room and maybe do some crunches to sweat off the heavy lunch. I was immediately called back, however. The 'Eating Disorder patients,' meaning my roommates and I, were not allowed to go to their room just yet. We needed to be under supervision for another fifteen minutes in order for them to make sure 'we would not do anything we shouldn't,' meaning throw up or exercise, or anything of that sort. With a sigh, I accepted my punishment, and we were ordered to sit on one of those hard chairs in the main nurses' office until fifteen minutes had passed and we were finally allowed to go.

I followed Becky back through the hall, Sara walking beside me in a mute statue-like shuffle. She showed no sign of life outside of the noiseless and inconceivable motions of her feet as she dragged herself along. How had she fallen so deep?

We arrived back at our room, where to my surprise I found a small child sitting on the side of my bed. She waved at me and motioned for me to come to her, which I could not refuse. I took several steps forward and bent down to face her.

"Hello," I said. "My name is Christina. Who are you?"

The girl did not reply. I sat down on the bed and allowed her to take one of my books from the bedside table. Her large curious eyes inspected the cover, and a frown appeared on her forehead as her fingers traced the title.

"It's French," I explained. "You might not understand it."

The girl took no note of my warning. She opened up the novel and started flipping through the pages, still refusing to say a word. I looked at Sara questioningly, yet she appeared as clueless as I was. I then let my gaze wander to Becky, who brought up her shoulders but then decided to elaborate nonetheless.

"Her name is Elyse," she explained. "She's the youngest girl here. Her father recently died in a car accident, and since then she has not said a word. Not even to her mother, with whom she was previously very close. Her mother is worried out of her wits, as you might have guessed."

My heart cramped together in pain. I wondered how *I* would feel if my father died in a car crash. I would be devastated. I would never be able to cope.

Maybe she saw the pain in my eyes or maybe it was all just coincidental, but at that moment Becky retreated, and I was left alone with Elyse. Except for Sara, of course, who was never really there anyway.

Suddenly I heard a ripping sound beside me. I turned my head and found Elyse clawing at the pages of my book.

"What the... no! Stop it. You can't do that, *please.*" I tried to take hold of her small prying hands, but she continued tearing at the pages. Her raving fingers hurled around like a lawnmower gone mad. "Don't. Please...."

After a moment of fight, I finally took hold of her hands, and she instantly let her body go limp. She fell against my chest while I took in the sight of the shredded pages. Elyse started to bawl, much like I wanted to do at the sight of my tattered refuge. My book, all ripped into pieces....

"You can't do something like that to other people's things, you know." I tried to explain. Elyse looked up at me and then back down at my lap.

"Books are sacred," I continued, "and they should be read rather than ripped."

I hesitantly let go of her hands, which she immediately clamped around my waist. In a nearby room, I could hear the drooling boy wail at the top of his lungs, causing Elyse to merely hold on to me tighter. She squeezed my waist as though her life depended on it, yanking so hard it felt uncomfortable. I tried to loosen up her grip, but to no avail. Sara simply watched the scene from her bed, dumbfounded and frozen stupid.

Several minutes had passed when finally a nurse arrived to take Elyse away.

"After lunch, patients are supposed to stay in their rooms until three o'clock," and she would not accept otherwise, no matter by whom. Grabbing Elyse by the hand and dragging her toward the door, the nurse turned back to face me one last time. She motioned her free hand up and down, indicating I should lie myself down on the bed. Her face was empty and her gesture crude, yet I did as I was told in order not to bring upon me another of her short-tempered outbursts. I'd already heard numerous of the nurses lose their temper in the brief period I had been here, and it honestly scared me all the way to my fragile bones. I did not want to fall victim to their short span of patience.

I sat up in bed and gathered my book pages, placing them neatly into my cabinet. My head still buzzing and my stomach turning queasily, I lay down and was carried off into a restless sleep.

When I woke up, the same boy I'd seen earlier was standing by the door of my room, staring in. He seemed to be around the same age I was, maybe slightly older. His brown curly hair fell in front of his green eyes, yet he did not brush it aside. He remained unmoving as he gazed, leaning against the wall with his hands beside his body.

Feeling uncomfortable being watched whilst having a nap, I straightened up in bed and quickly combed my hands through my hair. Beside me, Becky was reading and Sara remained peacefully asleep.

Upon my awakening, the boy came out of his magically frozen state and advanced. Still having a strangely churning feeling in the pit my stomach, I hesitantly introduced myself. What else was there to be done?

Upon my introduction, the boy's cheeks glowed and his face came alive. He reached out his hand, which I shook briefly.

"I'm Filip," her said. "I sleep in the room next door."

He gave me a timid smile, revealing shining metal braces. They gave him a sort of Middle School boyish kind of look, but he must have been around sixteen or seventeen years old. He was tall, incredibly tall, and his green eyes were curious yet somehow dulled. Acne covered his chin and forehead, and his Adam's apple protruded from his slender neck. His hand felt warm to my touch, and my fingertips tingled long after he let go. I couldn't help but smile as he clumsily sat down on the side of my bed while his gaze hesitantly remained on my face. Small dimples appeared on his cheeks and again he blushed slightly; the pinkish glow seemed to belong there, as though it did not want to leave once it had arrived.

After his short introduction and a moment of awkward silence, he opened up and cast me a glance into his life. His low voice rang between the walls of the room like music, resonating to fill up the cracks and hollow crevices. I felt at ease for the first time in quite a while, and I talked and talked to simply get everything off my chest. Eventually, however, we arrived at deeper waters. I knew it would come, that the curiosity would eventually get the upper hand, yet it felt strange to hear the words coming out of his mouth. He asked me why I was in the hospital, and I couldn't but reply truthfully to his puppy-eyed gaze.

"I... uh... Anorexia." I mumbled.

He nodded without making a fuss. Though I must have been lobster red, unable to breathe from apprehension, Filip merely accepted my answer in a way nobody else could have done, and I knew we were on the same boat. We were both outsiders.

"What about you?" I inquired. "Why are you here?"

He moved his arm onto the bed and revealed his bandaged wrist. I kept in the gasp that threatened to escape from my throat and shatter the tranquility.

"I tried to commit suicide," he said calmly. His face fell and I put my hand on his back, stroking it reassuringly. No more had to be said. He had just told me something of such a weight that no words could turn the atmosphere back around. Our silence spoke more than a thousand words. All I could think about was my own attempt at taking my life.

"Are you feeling any better? I mean... now, here?"

He moved his head back and forth slowly. "I've been here for two weeks already, but because they're changing my medication I have to stay longer. I am not allowed to go home yet, even though my mood has improved lately. I still feel really down sometimes."

I remained silent. I understood.

"Well, I have to go," he announced suddenly, standing up from the bed and reaching out his hand to me once again. "Visiting hour will be soon, and I'm sure a girl like you expects a visit."

I blushed at his remark and looked down at my hands. "I'm sure you'll a have visitor, too" I offered, but his expression conveyed that he did not.

"Oh. Uh.... Well, if I weren't here myself, I would come visit you."

His goofy smile returned to his face. "Thanks," he said as he waved me goodbye.

Less than half an hour later my father arrived for his visit.

CHAPTER NINETEEN

A week passed. I don't know how, but it did. Most of my days I spent reading and solving Sudoku puzzles, chatting with Becky and going to therapies, and each day before visiting hour I could expect Filip to come knocking on my door. This was the best therapy of all.

"Snack time!" The usual voice cut through the evening air to announce our desserts. Becky and I had been sitting on our beds, chatting on and on about her leaving the next day. She seemed super-excited, and so was I, though at the same time I knew I would miss her terribly much. Several of her goods had already been packed away, but her clothes still filled the cupboards and a stack of magazines remained on her bedside table.

Somehow, she did not seem ready to leave, even if her business here was finished and she would be gone before lunchtime tomorrow.

Becky and I made our way to the small kitchen, where we collected our puddings and joined the group of others at the long tables. I say puddings – *plural* – because, being Eating Disorder patients, we each got two. Some wicked method to speed up the weight gain.

Anyway, we ate our puddings in an uncommon silence, waited the desired fifteen minutes, and then made our way back to the bedroom. As usual, Sara was tongue-tied and a new eating disorder patient, Annette, did not say a word either. Becky and I returned to packing without following the majority of others to the game room for a lousy movie. They played a new one almost every night, so what did we care?

I passed Becky a stack of magazines while she pushed several of her clothes into her travel suitcase. Suddenly she looked up and I could see that tears had welled up in her eyes.

"What's wrong?" I asked. "Aren't you happy to be going home?"

She now smiled wryly back at me. "Of course I am happy to go home, but I'll no longer have the constant monitoring. I'm just afraid it will all repeat itself... worsen maybe. I'm just so worried"

I nodded knowingly. It dawned on me that I, too, would be facing the exact same thing, though I think going home would mostly just be a relief at this stage.

"Listen," I told her. "From the limited time that I've known you, I can say with confidence that your most prominent characteristic is your willpower – call it stubbornness if you like."

She allowed a hesitant giggle to chime into the air as I continued. "I know you can keep this up. I know you can fight your path all the way up to recovery. I just know you can."

She took the magazines from my outstretched hands and placed them haphazardly on top of her clothes. When she looked back up, a smile had returned to her face. We ended up going to see the lousy movie after all.

"Breakfast!" the shrill nurse's voice immediately awoke me from sleep. Two hours earlier I had been weighed, but I had dozed off again almost instantly afterwards, as was the case almost every morning.

I rubbed the sleep out of my eyes and quickly pulled a brush through my hair, yanking at the knots. I then rapidly joined the others at the breakfast table, where the blonde nurse was busily putting out the different plates. Everyone got their usual two slices of bread with a thick layer of cream cheese spreading. I got three.

"Excuse me?" I tapped the nurse on her shoulder. "I think you're mistaken, but I'm supposed to get two slices, not three."

The nurse looked at me skeptically, her thinly-drawn eyebrows moving down over her large black eyes. Her fine red-painted lips moved up into a half-smile.

"I'm sorry, Miss," she told me, "but they're doctor's orders. Dr. Paula has raised your portions."

My eyes nearly popped out of their sockets. Why hadn't Dr. Paula told me about this? She couldn't just go and change my meal plan whenever she wanted to! Although, well, maybe she could.

I ate two slices of bread and left the third one untouched. My "finished" plate was then returned to the nurse, who gave me a stern look. Giving her a daring glare in return, I remained silent and stubbornly held up my chin. She took the plate away without comment, and I was sure the topic would be brought up during the therapy later that day....

Suddenly I felt a pressure on my shoulder. It was Becky. Somehow, I had not noticed her absence throughout the meal, having been too preoccupied with the extra slice of bread I had received. I was about to wish her a good morning when I noticed the expression on her face. It wasn't her usual cheerful smile, her defined cheekbones not accentuated by the habitual grin.

"I'm leaving." The first thing she told me, and I replied with a mere "I know." A smile never once broke through on her features. Her face remained alarmingly empty, like a blank sheet of paper yet to be written upon.

"I'll be missing your company," her voice shook as she uttered the words. "But I'm sure we'll see each other again. Right?" She blinked several times in close succession.

"Of course we will," I reassured her, although I knew that she lived hours and hours away.

Becky looked over her shoulder and then back at me. "My mom is here to pick me up, so I guess I'll get going." She wiped her eyes with her sleeve and leaned down to hug me, after which a nurse led her to the entrance doors. Her sweet perfume lingered in my nostrils, and I could still feel her curls tickling my cheek. I followed her path with my eyes – walking that hallway and impatiently waiting for the door to be unlocked. I followed her all the way until she fell into her mother's arms at the other side, and I knew I would miss her. She was the only girl I'd had real contact with, and I wouldn't know what to do with myself without her. My eyes bade hers farewell as she looked around, waved weakly at me, and then was led off into the outside world. I never saw her again.

Later that day during therapy I told Dr. Paula about Becky's departure. With a mere shaking of the head she acknowledged my recollections, but she seemed uninvolved.

After having silently heard my longwinded narrations, she eventually spoke her mind, shattering the peace with her sharp tongue and strong accent. "If you continue your efforts, you too will be able to go home."

But that was not what I had meant. Not at all. On one side, yes, I did indeed want to get out, but on the other hand this idea frightened me to death. There was no point discussing this with her, however. She wouldn't understand.

I thus simply nodded at her statement, letting my mind wander elsewhere while the therapy struggled its way through time.

* * *

At around two o'clock in the afternoon I was distracted from my book by the familiar knock on the door. Filip walked in and sat down on the side of my bed as had turned into a habit by now. He smiled down at me gently, and I sat up in bed and pressed my knees to my chest. I stretched out my arms and stroked his hand gently, my eyes remaining on his statue-like face. He peered at me through his lashes, observing me as if I was a piece of art, and the intensity of it extracted a smile on my lips. It felt as natural to me as the start of a new day, the driving away of night.

My dad could not come visit me today because of a meeting (though I expected this meeting had more to do with Miriam than anything else), and Filip and I talked until the sun had started its descent.

"So..." I asked him, cutting through the comfortable silence that hung between us, allowing an even more pleasant sound to fill the atmosphere. "If you don't mind my curiosity, why are you only so seldom visited? I mean, don't your parents come by, or your friends? Your girlfriend?"

It was okay for me to ask. We'd discussed so much already, dug so deep that I knew this would not come as an intrusion to his privacy.

He smiled sadly, but explained confidently. "My parents are busy. We live two hours away from the hospital, so it's rather inconvenient for them to have to drive here and back every day. I didn't tell my friends about what happened. It would be a bit... uncomfortable. And I don't have a girlfriend."

My heart jumped upon hearing this.

"And you?" he now confronted me. "Do you have a boyfriend?"

I blushed. Did this conversation really need to take this turn? How could I explain to him that I did indeed have a boyfriend – or, well, at least a boy who expected me to return his love once I got out of here?

"I... uh... yes. Yes, I do. Have a boyfriend, I mean." Upon saying this I expected Filip to flinch back, to crawl into himself like a turtle in its shell, to do *anything* that could possibly betray that he cared. But he didn't.

His expected reaction stayed off. He seemed neither disappointed nor surprised, and his crooked half-smile never once threatened to leave his face. It made it easier on me, yet at the same time it made it all the more difficult. I would not have to deal with an impossible lover, yet at the same time I craved the tenderness it could bring.

I guess it made sense all the same, but I just longed so much for people to tell me they cared about me and loved me for who I was. I needed to feel special, that's all.

Whatever it did bring about, Filip's reaction certainly did not give me that special feeling I so craved. If anything, his face only brightened further. In his eyes, however, I detected a minute alteration. They seemed to shimmer in the light, almost like the moist shine of drizzle on the morning leaves.

A sad smile came over my lips as I sought his gaze, yet his eyes remained cast down onto the bed.

"I have to go," he said, and he resolutely stood up, eyeballing the large clock above the door. Without allowing me time for a response, he disappeared from the room. I lay down in bed and wept silently.

* * *

After dinner Dr. Paula came to get me.

"I'm sorry for the late therapy," she apologized. "But it has been an incredibly busy day."

She held her hands in front of her and sort of waved them around in circular motions. I guess it was supposed to be some sort of apologetic gesture, yet it looked rather awkward to see her flail her arms around like a flopping fish out of the water. One thing was sure, though: she certainly seemed rushed. Her hair fell in strands around her head and she panted softly. It was certainly no reason for her to apologize to me though, as I had all the time in the world on my hands anyway. It didn't matter to me when we'd have our therapy, whether it be early morning or late at night.

"It's okay," I assured her. "It's nice to see you."

She hardly acknowledged my words as she impatiently tapped her foot on the floor tiles, waiting for me to put my book aside and get out of bed. She led me through the hall and to the large entrance, where she nervously tried all her keys. A sigh of frustration left through her clenched teeth as the metal clashed together, creating a shrill rasp like that of nails on a chalkboard. She took out the last of her keys and pushed open the door. I followed her to her office in a half-run, not daring to shuffle behind. She left the door open for me as she sat down in her usual fauteuil, her leg hopping up and down, less fervently now than before. I found my chair and noiselessly sat down on it, feeling the peace slowly return with the familiar scenery.

Dr. Paula took a deep breath and, as if she had not just hopped around like Alice in Wonderland's time-obsessed White Rabbit, she now calmly placed her hands onto her lap and commenced.

"The last couple of weeks we mostly talked about you and the possible reasons for the development of your eating disorder. Today, we will take a slightly different approach. In the next couple of sessions, we will do some further self-exploration through art."

I raised my eyebrows, yet she ignored the gesture.

"I am going to ask you to draw two different trees. One will have to be a fruit tree – any fruit tree you like – and the second should be a tree taken right from your fantasy – anything is possible."

Her voice trailed off as she stood up from her couch and confidently strode to her desk, from which she took a cup full of colored pencils. Leaving the drawer still half-open, she walked to the right of the room, where she conjured two clean white printer papers. She placed the items in front of me.

"I'll give you some time. Take as long as you need." With these words, she turned around to start up her computer, which came to life with a hum. The room filled with a roaring chaos, yet Dr. Paula, probably used to the noise, simply sat down in her office chair and resumed her activity.

On the one hand, I liked the fact that she gave me the privacy to deal with this on my own, but on the other hand I had no idea how to proceed. Draw a tree? What good would that going do?

Though seeing no clear point, I did as I was told, first carefully sketching an apple tree and then making another tree that yielded heart-shaped fruits. Because the doctor seemed impatient at me 'taking my time,' I hurried up a little, while at the same time making my drawings as neat as possible.

When I was done, Dr. Paula took the papers from me and shortly glanced them over. She then put them back on the table and turned to face me.

"Interesting," she mumbled, shoving my first piece sideways for us to both see it well. "Would you like to know what I'm taking away from this? There is a lot I can learn from this drawing."

I nodded. I honestly had no idea, but it sounded interesting enough.

Dr. Paula scanned over the drawing anew. "Lets start with the trunk. It's what the tree needs to stand – without it, it wouldn't be a tree, strong and majestic, as it is now."

I rolled my eyes at her vague statements, but she continued. "The trunk you drew is rather thin. This could indicate that you don't feel very strong – a heavy wind could snap you at a weakness." To emphasize her words, she snapped her fingers.

I looked at the doctor questioningly, but her eyes were glued to the drawing.

"The roots, the branches... there are none visible at all. The roots and branches generally indicate a person's relationships with family and friends, yet in this case it appears they are nonexistent. I've had several therapies with you before, however, and I know this might not be true in your case. It could possibly indicate the blow your trust has gotten when the bullying commenced."

I fumbled with the sleeves of my sweater, not really liking the way the conversation was turning. How could she make all of that up simply by looking at a meaningless drawing? On the other hand, her comments did seem to describe my situation. I shrugged – it was probably just luck.

"Next, I also see your tree is placed perfectly in the center of the page, which means you are living in the now, and—"

"Excuse me," I interrupted. "But what would it otherwise indicate? I mean, if the tree had either been placed more to the left... or the right?"

Dr. Paula had not expected this question, but, folding her hands in her lap, she looked back at me and explained, "On the left of the page indicates living in the past; on the right means living in the future."

Though some of her previous points had seemed to make at least some sense, this observation seemed simply absurd. Whether the tree was located on the right, left, or middle – what did that matter? I lived in the present simply because the location of a tree said so? Ridiculous!

The doctor ignored my doubts over her fortune-telling skills and animatedly continued her explanation, this time focusing on the fruits growing in the tree.

"You chose apples," she stated plainly. "Apples are commonly chosen. Your apples are hanging from the tree in quite a symmetrical way. Appealing to the eye. Aesthetically pleasing. You like clear rules and guidelines, perfection in all the little things."

I did not reply, instead resting my gaze on the tissue box on the center table. It was decorated with daisies that, as a result of the blurriness and filters, looked like their carpels were faces with downward-pointing pouts. They all looked so miserable, so taunting, that I leaned forward and moved the box onto the floor to my right, beside the couch, so I wouldn't have to look at it anymore.

Dr. Paula observed at me knowingly. "That is exactly what I mean. Everything has to be a certain way – it's some sort of obsessive-compulsive disorder."

I objected. "But—"

"And the surface below your tree!" Dr. Paula was now shouting. "You made no grass or sand or anything for your tree to stand on. Why not?"

She looked at me with accusing eyes that seemed to pierce right into my soul. I quickly cast down my glance.

"Why I didn't make a ground?" I muttered. The situation was almost comical. "Why... I guess I probably forgot. What importance does it have anyway?"

She looked at me in shock. "*What importance does it have?* It has *huge* importance! The floor stands for your confidence and ties with the world. Not having any could indicate you don't really feel home, or it could indicate you might have had suicidal thoughts... Have you had any of those recently?"

Her red face turned worried, and I rapidly shook my head.

"Good," she concluded, but her face remained grave. Her eye twitched uncomfortably as she noticed another feature on my drawing.

"What?" I asked, but her eyes were focused on a single point. "What is it?"

Her gaze slowly travelled up toward my face, and she stared at me blankly while her finger moved over the trunk of the tree.

"You made a hole here. Such a cavity is... it means... a tree hole indicates a serious trauma." And once again, I was forced to dig deeply into my past.

CHAPTER TWENTY

Today the usual knocking at my door did not come as a relief. Lunch had taken place a little over two hours earlier, but I could still feel the heavy lump in my stomach. I had been unable to finish my meal, but the nurse had made me stay at the table until all had been finished. Filip had wanted to wait beside me loyally, yet the nurse had sent him away. She had stared at my plate until all had disappeared, after which the fifteen minutes of waiting time seemed like an hour. When I finally arrived in my room, I wished there be mirrors around – I needed to have a look at my changing body, which now seemed completely out of my control. Not a single mirror was to be found anywhere in the psychiatric ward, however. I instead decided to get some rest, yet even this did not give my mind any peace.

The knocking at my door did not come as a relief. As soon as I saw Filip's face I knew something was up. My roommates – two new girls who seldom said a word – curiously took in the newcomer, inspecting him with hungry eyes that made me quiver apprehensively. He wasn't there to be shared.

Filip, his head cast down as though avoiding eye contact, shuffled his way to the bed and sat down. His visiting ritual had been put on hold for the past week, and I had the eerie sense that it wasn't because of unfortunate therapy scheduling.

He was here now, however, and I was both happy and worried at the same time. His green eyes were aimed at the floor and his shoulders were slumped. My heart fluttered at the thought that something was wrong.

Filip moved around on the side of the bed to position his body more openly toward me. His gaze moved up over my body and to my face, where they remained. He opened his mouth to speak, but then resolutely closed it again. I waited patiently until he was ready, which eventually he was. He came right to the point, yet what he had to say was not at all like anything I'd expected. The words he uttered slapped me in the face like a morning alarm wake-up call.

"I... uh... I'm going to Croatia for two weeks for the holidays."

A weak smile came over his lips, and I painted a hesitant one onto my face as well.

"That's *great*," I mimed. "Aren't you excited about it?"

He straightened his black sweater and pulled on the sleeves nervously. The sheepish smile partially returned to his countenance, and his mouth curled up slightly. He observed my face, scrupulously surveying my reaction, yet I would not let any emotion seep through to betray myself. When he spoke, the words forming on his lips like the pure drops of dew, my ears were like guards that forbade any of them to pass me by.

"Well, yes, of course I'm excited. I just... I'll have to come back. And I'll be leaving you here practically by yourself."

"Is that what you're worried about?" I exclaimed. I laughed at the irony, and he, too, seemed to lose some of his tension. He nodded frantically, and we both burst out in a fit of nervous giggles.

"It's okay, silly," I assured him. "I won't run away. I'll be right here when you return."

A sigh escaped from my lips with difficulty, and his green eyes drowned me as I spoke the last words. "I'll be okay, silly. I'll be okay."

He leaned forward and his face came closer to my own. Our noses were practically touching and I could feel his breath on my skin. My heart pounded loudly in my chest and I stubbornly pushed back the thought of him leaving. I cast down my head and felt myself get lost in his embrace, unwilling to let go. I wanted the hug to last forever, yet before I was fully aware of it, Filip had left the bed and I sat alone. I looked up at the door just in time to catch a last glimpse of his back. Several minutes later I heard the shrill voice of a nurse echo through the hallway, and Filip rushed by, looking around several times to catch my eye. I heard a key twist in the lock and Filip dashed off.

CHAPTER TWENTY-ONE

Several more people left the hospital that Sunday, and it was only a matter of time before a new load would arrive. For now, however, all was frighteningly still, outside of the soft classical music floating from the bedroom to my left. I made my way to the small bathroom, my cold feet stuck into slippers and my arms clumsily struggling to keep hold of my clothes, a towel, and several shower products. I shuffled toward the with-stickers-decorated door and pushed down the handle with my elbow. I nudged the door open by leaning my weight against it and then quickly stepped into the small area.

Dropping my belongings in the corner of the room, I stripped down and stepped into the open shower area. There was no lock on the door, so I rapidly disappeared behind the ledge of the stone wall. I turned on the water and waited for it to heat up before stepping underneath the warm stream. It felt good to be clean, and I massaged the soft foamy shower gel into my skin in slow circular motions. When reaching my breasts, I stopped momentarily to look down. My body had grown to a new proportion, yet my breasts had yet to follow. My hands moved down over my stomach to my hips, where they then took repose. Though my angular hips were still prominently visible, they were no longer the sharp pointy edges I had had earlier. Disappointing.

Once again I cursed the fact that there was not a mirror to be found. I bent down to squeeze a daub of shampoo into my hands and massaged the gel into my hair as the hot water continued to roll down my back. My eyes remained down, and I let them travel slowly over my body, now resting on my thighs. The ugly scarred tissue reminded me of my former life – a life that now seemed so far away it appeared to be somebody else's entirely.

Something like that couldn't have happened to me, it simply couldn't.

I stepped back into the stream of water and let it wash off my pain, let it seep away into the drain and be gone.

Taking my towel from the pile, I quickly dried off and changed, my wet hair leaving a dark stain at the back of my shirt.

* * *

"Christina! You have a visitor!"

I rushed through the hall toward the door, excited to see my dad outside of his usual twice-or-thrice a week visit. I was happily surprised, which had probably been his intention. I twisted a lock of hair between my thumb and index as the door was opened for me. My foot thumped impatiently up and down on the tiles.

When the door swung open, the nurse nudged me out into the visiting area – an enclosed space with a large window that looked out into another section of the building. Also locked, of course.

"Hey."

I recognized the voice before I saw the all-too-familiar face. My heart stood still and I almost turned back around when he stopped me, placing his warm hand on my shoulder.

"Christina." Marc looked down into my eyes to keep my attention. "Your father told me you were here.... Didn't you get my messages? You need to understand that you are not to blame for this, and neither am I." He towered above me and placed both hands on my shoulders. He shook me slightly, cautiously, as though I came from another planet and was to be handled with care.

"No... no...." I murmured, my nails digging into my palms as I balled my knuckles. "I am to blame. I am responsible for my own actions and –"

"Stop it," he cut me off. "Sit down."

I wanted to protest, but a sudden weakness seized control over my body. Marc held his hand invitingly over the red couch, on which I dutifully sat down. He let himself fall back in the soft seat as well, but I had no intention to get myself as comfortable as he did. I remained at the edge of the seat, ready to jump up at any moment.

"Relax," Marc mumbled. "I've missed you."

His sincere eyes looked into mine and I could feel something break inside of me. Marc....

"It's okay," I stuttered, "I missed you too. I missed you a lot."

He looked directly at me and placed his clammy hand onto my cheek, stroking my hair back with the other.

"Geez, Christina, I can see your cheekbones. You really are too thin."

I wanted to change the subject, his concern wouldn't do any good, but his eyes were already trailing down my body. I consciously zipped up my sweater and interlocked my hands in front of me, yet his eyes continues their path.

"You're like a walking skeleton." He laughed at his own joke. "You really should eat. As soon as you're out of here we'll go out for some big greasy burgers. Extra fries."

I looked at him in a haze; my vision was blurred. Was he serious?

"I... I don't think that's such a great idea —"

"Of course it is."

I fumbled with the red cloth of the couch, twisting it between my fingers anxiously. I couldn't do this, just wasn't strong enough to. Why could he not just accept this?

"I just..."

"Just trust me. It's a great idea and –"

This was the last straw. It wasn't "a great idea" as he claimed, and he should look through his own selfishness into the real world. Could he not see my pain seeping through the pores of my skin and begging him to shut up for just one moment?

"No, it's not! Just listen to me, please. I can't. Not yet...."

I couldn't help but think of Filip, who would never have said something as thoughtless as that. The smirk disappeared from Marc's face as he took both my hands into his. "I'm sorry, baby. I didn't mean to upset you."

I cast down my glance. "It's okay. You couldn't have known."

"It's just... have you not seen that movie with that live skeleton?" A tentative smile appeared on his face, but when he saw my discomfort it quickly faded away. Did he really...?

I stood up without saying another word, intent on knocking on the door for the nurse to let me back in. Before my knuckles even reached the wood, however, Marc put his hand on my shoulder and soothed me back to the sofa. Numbed with pain, I let him pull the strings. Inside, I was crying.

About 45 minutes after the arrival of my guest, the nurse finally came back to return me to the department. It seemed like a lifetime had passed.

"I hope we're okay now." Marc muttered. "I have to go, but I'll miss you. Keep fighting."

He placed a swift kiss onto my lips and enclosed me in an embrace. I sighed as I was taken in by his warmth. When his arms let go of my posture, he once again pressed his mouth onto mine, and I felt his greedy tongue push in between my lips. It felt different than it used to. The understanding was gone.

The nurse let Marc out of the visiting area, and he slumped into the waiting elevator without once looking over his shoulder at me. I meekly waved at the back that never turned.

The nurse unlocked the second door that let me into the department, and I willingly entered. As soon as the door had opened before me, I rushed to my bedroom, where another stern nurse prohibited me from entering. I was at the verge of tears, yet protest was futile.

"It's dinner time. No more going into rooms – you're already late."

With my head down, I strolled toward the dinner table, on which was served an undistinguishable mash of overcooked spaghetti and rubbery vegetables. My portion was huge and cold, but I wouldn't let my fear show. Bravely, I advanced upon the metal cart on which the eating utensils were placed. Leaning forward to take out a knife and fork, the same stout nurse who had prevented me going into my room slapped me on the fingers.

"No knife for you today," she told me while handing me a fork and a spoon.

"But I always eat spaghetti with a fork and knife. Could I just –"

"No. No, you cannot," she cut me off, redirecting me to my seat.

Without saying a word and with the harsh look of the nurse remaining upon me, I ate my meal and was eventually able to return to my room. I was nauseous and melancholic, and, after having changed into my pajamas, almost immediately dozed off into a feverish sleep.

CHAPTER TWENTY-TWO

Marc's visit had taken place over two weeks earlier, and I could feel my mental state improve finally. Though prohibited from knowing my weight, I could see the nurse smile at me as she recorded the numbers each morning. She told me all was well, but more she could not say.

Filip had returned from Croatia. He told me about the great time he'd had there with his mom, and he seemed much happier than the last time I had seen him. As he had to change his medication yet again, he needed to stay in the hospital for several more weeks, but after that he would be able to go home. I had smiled at the words that joyfully rolled off his lips, which had not stood still once since he had returned. The routine daily visits recommenced as if he had never left. It was as though the Croatian sun still reflected in his grinning face, blocking out the horrific thoughts I had once possessed. It felt great.

Today, however, I was anxious, apprehensive for what was to come. I tidied my bed for the third time that morning, folding the blanket double in order to make it look as though it was properly made up. I took the picture frame my father had given me from the bedside table and pushed it on top of the clothes inside my over-full-bag. Life around me continued while I impatiently stumbled around the room.

Maneuvering my arm into my bag, I pulled out my book. I was too tense, my head was everywhere at once, and I needed to calm myself down. My mind had to have some peace – to trail away at least for the moment.

I sank deeply into the pillow and opened the novel, flipping the pages between my fingers. The familiar shuffling sound and dusty smell filled me with warmth and nostalgia, and I let myself be carried away. Momentarily.

It felt nice to disappear, letting the hospital noises and activities simply pass me by without acknowledging them, yet that did not stop me from having to read the same page three times in order for the words to truly sink in. I was carried away, though only partially, into a magical land where I was not truly myself at all.

I heard the knocking at my door and was immediately ripped away from my book. It shamed me to have been so eagerly awaiting his arrival, but I couldn't help the beat my heart skipped whenever I thought of him. I knew it was wrong.

"Hi." Filip sat down at the edge of my bed. "Your dad will probably arrive real soon. I still can't believe you're leaving. I just came to say my proper goodbye."

My eyes glided out the window and then back toward his face. His braces glistened as he gave me a mischievous grin, and he placed his soft hand on my shoulder, making me incapable of forming a response.

"Last week, in Croatia, I bought you this necklace." He held the shiny silver in the light.

I bundled up my hair with quivering hands and leaned forward. Filip tenderly enclosed the jewel around my neck, fumbling with the lock. The small blue stone was cool on my chest, and I put my hands on the material to feel its smooth surface.

"It looks nice," he told me. "It really does. Especially now that your face is... fuller. You look pretty. Beautiful."

"Thank you," I muttered, taken by the sudden confession. "Thanks a lot. It really means a lot." My stomach turned, but from excitement rather than fear.

"I just –"

"Shhhh," he told me, placing his finger over his lips. "It's okay."

He leaned forward and I cast my head down when we made eye contact. He wrapped his arms around me like a warm blanket on a winter night, and we remained that way until I discerned an unexpected movement at the door. I looked up to find Marc.

The bouquet of red roses in his hands swayed dangerously as he nearly dropped them to the floor. "I came to get you. Your dad thought you might have liked it if I picked you up, but I guess he was wrong."

His face was devoid of color, and a blue vain near his temple clearly stood out. He turned around to leave, but I called for him to stay.

"Marc! Why are you leaving? Wait for me. It's not what you think. We're, uh, just friends. Just wait for me, will you?"

He took a step back and remained disquietingly still while I picked up my bags from the floor. In the corner of my eye, I saw Filip's face fall. His gaze remained trained on an invisible speck of dust at his feet.

With my bag over my shoulder I made several steps toward the door and then paused. Marc sighed audibly.

I cast a last glance back at Filip, but he did not look up. I waved my hand at him in a gesture of goodbye, yet he hardly made any response at all. Holding my head low and mumbling some farewells to the nurses, I shuffled after Marc to the end of the hall, down the stairs, and out the building. He helped me load my belongings into his car without saying a word, and then he drove me home in further silence. Before letting me out, however, he placed his hand on top of mine and looked me right in the eye.

"Listen Christina. I just want you to know that it is okay if you had an affair. I understand, and I forgive you."

My eyebrows shot up in surprise. An affair? Me? I didn't...

"Yes, I know. It's not always easy to remain faithful, especially when you're there all by yourself. I have to admit, I have had my own moment of infidelity, but now we're quit. It's okay, you know. I'm sure it has brought us closer together and all." His eyes were hard blue marbles. "I'm sure it has made us stronger. Don't you agree?"

Not knowing how to respond to his revelation, I bobbed my head up and down. Simultaneously, Marc grasped for my hand and leaned in for a kiss. I made no attempt to move as he pressed his lips forcibly against mine, not giving me the opportunity to speak or breathe. When he let go, I fumbled to open the car door.

"Thanks for the drive," I muttered. I took out my bags from the trunk and stumbled my way to the house, ringing the bell that had by now lost its familiarity. My dad opened with an all-knowing smile.

"I see you two have missed each other," indicating the kiss he had overlooked from the kitchen window. "It's nice to have you back."

I fell into his arms and broke down.

* * *

August 3rd, 2009
Dear Diary,

Today was beyond anything I could have expected. I finally gained enough courage, and after breakfast I left the house and biked the long way to the Semmelai hospital. My heart was beating in my chest like the pounding feet of an elephant on the run, and my breathing came quickly and heavily as though I had just ran a marathon. It was not from exhaustion.

Upon arriving at the hospital I had a strong urge to return home, to simply jump onto my bike and drive all the way back. But I had not come for nothing. I wouldn't leave without at least having spoken my mind. I rang the bell at the entrance of the psychiatric ward and was let in by the smiling blonde-haired nurse. She greeted me kindly, telling me it was not actually allowed for me to visit outside of the prescribed time, but that she would close an eye to it for once. She winked at me and asked me whom I wished to see.

When I entered the ward I was overpowered with emotions. All the memories flooded over me at once, yet the nurse did not grant me time to recompose myself. I was led immediately to the room that, as I now realized, I had never before actually entered. I knocked out of custom, after which I hesitantly pushed open the door. Filip was alone in his room, and I went to sit on the side of his bed. He resumed his staring out the window, yet I noticed his face softened when I placed my cold hand on top of his.

"Filip," my voice shook, yet I was determined to prevail. "Filip... I told you I would come visit you had I not been stuck inside the hospital myself, didn't I?"

He looked at me and nodded, his eyes glazed over as he thought back of the conversation that now seemed to have taken place ages ago.

"Of course I remember," he replied. "How could I have forgotten?"

The familiar grin come over his lips.

"Well, here I am." I laughed, still slightly uncomfortable.

His hesitant smile faded away again, and the dreaded question, pronounced in an almost casual manner, hung between us like a heavy blanket that deprived the room of its oxygen. "So, how is Marc?"

My eyes sought his, but he had gone back to staring out the window.

"Marc is.... Marc is past tense."

His eyes immediately returned to my face and his baffled look extracted a giggle from my lips. "Yes. You heard that well."

"Does that mean —" he started, but I broke him off.

"Shhhh," I whispered, placing my fingers on my lips. "It does indeed."

I let myself fall into his arms and be carried away by his touch. When he kissed me, it was a feeling that would never leave me again, and my heart was filled with an unknown yet immediately accepted warmth. I knew I had made the right decision, and I knew that I would help him throughout his healing process as he would with mine.

An involuntary smile came over my lips as he whispered in my ear. "Don't let anyone bring you down again, because they're really not worth your time. You are worth it and that's all that matters."

By this time my eyes had filled up with tears, but he was not done yet.

"Christina..." he mumbled. "You are perfect to me. Just perfect."

Christina

ABOUT THE AUTHOR

Hanne Arts is an eighteen-year-old budding author, recipient of the Short List Award in 2011, Honorable Mention in 2012, and Second Place in 2013 in the Short Story Competition Hungary. She was shortlisted in the Nancy Thorp Poetry Competition in 2013 and Junior Author Short Story Competition in 2014.

Hanne currently lives in Slovakia, and has previously lived in Belgium, Holland and Hungary. She wrote this novel in the hope of helping others struggling with depression and eating disorders understand that they are not alone, and that they, too, can overcome their inner demons. For more information, visit www.hanne-arts.blogspot.sk and check out her Facebook page.

CPSIA information can be obtained at www.ICGtesting.com
Printed in the USA
BVOW08s2154210915

419031BV00002B/15/P